Social Satire and
the Modern Novel

This edition is dedicated to Bonnie Stabile,
voracious reader and able editor

Social Satire and the Modern Novel

Arnold Bennett's
Buried Alive

Edited and introduced by
Paul Rich

WESTPHALIA PRESS
An imprint of Policy Studies Organization

Social Satire and the Modern Novel
Arnold Bennett's *Buried Alive*

Westphalia Press
An imprint of Policy Studies Organization
dgutierrezs@ipsonet.org

For information:
Westphalia Press
1527 New Hampshire Ave., N.W.
Washington, D.C. 20036

ISBN-13: 978-1-935907-02-2
ISBN-10: 1935907026

Updated material and comments on this edition can be found
at the Policy Studies Organization website:
http://www.ipsonet.org/

PREFACE TO THIS EDITION

ARNOLD Bennett (1867-1931) came from a modest background in Hanley, England. He was an assistant editor for a woman's magazine until his novels achieved success and he was able to move to Paris in 1903, where he won acceptance in French cultural circles. *Buried Alive* appeared in 1908 when his reputation was cresting.

An Arnold Bennett Society is devoted to his work, publishing a newsletter and arranging various anniversary celebrations, at some of which the dish Omelette Arnold Bennett is served. This is a dish that includes haddock and Hollandaise sauce and which was first served at the Savoy Hotel in London, and is still on the menu.

E

Buried Alive is not a Count Dracula horror story. Rather, it is a comic novel that concerns a painter, Priam Farll, whose shyness is overcome by love, and whose life is muddled by mistaken identity. Frank Harris (1856-1931) was editor of Vanity Fair and when *Buried Alive* appeared he wrote to Bennett (12 November 1908), "All my last hours in Paris were taken up with reading the book you gave my wife, "Buried Alive"...No laugher in Dickens at all like it, not of the same quality. It is more like Cervantes at his best." That may be extravagant, but there is no doubt that Bennett provides even after all the years a "jolly good read."

Paul Rich

BURIED ALIVE

A TALE OF THESE DAYS

BY

ARNOLD BENNETT

AUTHOR OF "THE GRAND BABYLON HOTEL," ETC.

COPYRIGHT EDITION

BRENTANO'S

NEW YORK.

Printed in Germany.

CONTENTS.

BURIED ALIVE.

———

CHAPTER I.

THE PUCE DRESSING-GOWN.

THE peculiar angle of the earth's axis to the plane of the ecliptic—that angle which is chiefly responsible for our geography and therefore for our history—had caused the phenomenon known in London as summer. The whizzing globe happened to have turned its most civilised face away from the sun, thus producing night in Selwood Terrace, South Kensington. In No. 91 Selwood Terrace two lights, on the ground-floor and on the first-floor, were silently proving that man's ingenuity can outwit nature's. No. 91 was one of about ten thousand similar houses between South Kensington Station and North End Road. With its grimy stucco front, its cellar kitchen, its hundred stairs and steps, its perfect inconvenience, and its conscience heavy with the doing to death of sundry general servants, it uplifted

tin chimney-cowls to heaven and gloomily awaited the
day of judgment for London houses, sublimely ignoring
the axial and orbital velocities of the earth and even
the reckless flight of the whole solar system through
space. You felt that No. 91 was unhappy, and that it
could only be rendered happy by a "To let" standard
in its front patch and a "No bottles" card in its cellar-
windows. It possessed neither of these specifics.
Though of late generally empty, it was never untenanted. In the entire course of its genteel and commodious career it had never once been to let.

Go inside, and breathe its atmosphere of a bored
house that is generally empty yet never untenanted.
All its twelve rooms dark and forlorn, save two; its
cellar kitchen dark and forlorn; just these two rooms,
one on the top of the other like boxes, pitifully struggling against the inveterate gloom of the remaining ten!
Stand in the dark hall and get this atmosphere into
your lungs.

The principal, the startling thing in the illuminated
room on the ground-floor was a dressing-gown, of the
colour, between heliotrope and purple, known to a previous generation as puce; a quilted garment stuffed with
swansdown, light as hydrogen—nearly, and warm as
the smile of a kind heart; old, perhaps, possibly worn
in its outlying regions and allowing fluffs of feathery
white to escape through its satin pores; but a dressing-

gown to dream of. It dominated the unkempt, naked
apartment, its voluptuous folds glittering crudely under
the sun-replacing oil lamp which was set on a cigar-box
on the stained deal table. The oil lamp had a glass
reservoir, a chipped chimney, and a cardboard shade,
and had probably cost less than a florin; five florins
would have purchased the table; and all the rest of the
furniture, including the armchair in which the dressing-
gown reclined, a stool, an easel, three packets of
cigarettes and a trouser-stretcher, might have been replaced for another ten florins. Up in the corners of the
ceiling, obscure in the eclipse of the cardboard shade,
was a complicated system of cobwebs to match the dust
on the bare floor.

Within the dressing-gown there was a man. This
man had reached the interesting age. I mean the age
when you think you have shed all the illusions of in-
fancy, when you think you understand life, and when
you are often occupied in speculating upon the delicious
surprises which existence may hold for you; the age, in
sum, that is the most romantic and tender of all ages
—for a male. I mean the age of fifty. An age absurdly misunderstood by all those who have not
reached it! A thrilling age! Appearances are tragic-
ally deceptive.

The inhabitant of the puce dressing-gown had a
short greying beard and moustache; his plenteous hair

was passing from pepper into salt; there were many
minute wrinkles in the hollows between his eyes and
the fresh crimson of his cheeks; and the eyes were sad;
they were very sad. Had he stood erect and looked
perpendicularly down, he would have perceived, not his
slippers, but a protuberant button of the dressing-gown.
Understand me: I conceal nothing; I admit the figures
written in the measurement-book of his tailor. He was
fifty. Yet, like most men of fifty, he was still very
young, and, like most bachelors of fifty, he was rather
helpless. He was quite sure that he had not had the
best of luck. If he had excavated his soul he would
have discovered somewhere in its deeps a wistful, ap-
pealing desire to be taken care of, to be sheltered from
the inconveniences and harshness of the world. But he
would not have admitted the discovery. A bachelor of
fifty cannot be expected to admit that he resembles a
girl of nineteen. Nevertheless it is a strange fact that
the resemblance between the heart of an experienced,
adventurous bachelor of fifty and the simple heart of a
girl of nineteen is stronger than girls of nineteen
imagine; especially when the bachelor of fifty is sitting
solitary and unfriended at two o'clock in the night, in
the forlorn atmosphere of a house that has outlived its
hopes. Bachelors of fifty alone will comprehend me.

It has never been decided what young girls do
meditate upon when they meditate; young girls them-

selves cannot decide. As a rule the lonely fancies of
middle-aged bachelors are scarcely less amenable to de-
finition. But the case of the inhabitant of the puce
dressing-gown was an exception to the rule. He knew,
and he could have said, precisely what he was thinking
about. In that sad hour and place, his melancholy
thoughts were centred upon the resplendent, unique
success in life of a gifted and glorious being known to
nations and newspapers as Priam Farll.

RICHES AND RENOWN.

In the days when the New Gallery was new, a
picture, signed by the unknown name of Priam Farll,
was exhibited there, and aroused such terrific interest
that for several months no conversation among cultured
persons was regarded as complete without some reference to it. That the artist was a very great painter
indeed was admitted by everyone; the only question
which cultured persons felt it their duty to settle was
whether he was the greatest painter that ever lived or
merely the greatest painter since Velasquez. Cultured
persons might have continued to discuss that nice point
to the present hour, had it not leaked out that the
picture had been refused by the Royal Academy. The
culture of London then at once healed up its strife and
combined to fall on the Royal Academy as an institu-

tion which had no right to exist. The affair even got
into Parliament and occupied three minutes of the imperial legislature. Useless for the Royal Academy to
argue that it had overlooked the canvas, for its dimensions were seven feet by five; it represented a policeman, a simple policeman, life-size, and it was not merely
the most striking portrait imaginable, but the first appearance of the policeman in great art; criminals, one
heard, instinctively fled before it. No! The Royal
Academy really could not argue that the work had
been overlooked. And in truth the Royal Academy did
not argue accidental negligence. It did not argue
about its own right to exist. It did not argue at all.
It blandly went on existing, and taking about a hundred and fifty pounds a day in shillings at its polished
turnstiles. No details were obtainable concerning Priam
Farll, whose address was Poste Restante, St. Martin's-
le-Grand. Various collectors, animated by deep faith
in their own judgment and a sincere desire to encourage
British art, were anxious to purchase the picture for a
few pounds, and these enthusiasts were astonished and
pained to learn that Priam Farll had marked a figure
of £1,000—the price of a rare postage stamp.

In consequence the picture was not sold; and after
an enterprising journal had unsuccessfully offered a reward for the identification of the portrayed policeman,
the matter went gently to sleep while the public em-

ployed its annual holiday as usual in discussing the big
gooseberry of matrimonial relations.

Everyone naturally expected that in the following
year the mysterious Priam Farll would, in accordance
with the universal rule for a successful career in British
art, contribute another portrait of another policeman to
the New Gallery—and so on for about twenty years, at
the end of which period England would have learnt to
recognise him as its favourite painter of policemen.
But Priam Farll contributed nothing to the New Gallery.
He had apparently forgotten the New Gallery; which
was considered to be ungracious, if not ungrateful, on
his part. Instead, he adorned the Paris salon with a
large seascape showing penguins in the foreground.
Now these penguins became the penguins of the continental year; they made penguins the fashionable bird
in Paris, and also (twelve months later) in London.
The French Government offered to buy the picture on
behalf of the Republic at its customary price of five
hundred francs, but Priam Farll sold it to the American
connoisseur Whitney C. Whitt for five thousand dollars.
Shortly afterwards he sold the policeman, whom he had
kept by him, to the same connoisseur for ten thousand
dollars. Whitney C. Whitt was the expert who had
paid two hundred thousand dollars for a Madonna and
St. Joseph, with donor, of Raphael. The enterprising
journal before mentioned calculated that, counting the

space actually occupied on the canvas by the policeman, the daring connoisseur had expended two guineas
per square inch on the policeman.

At which stage the vast newspaper public suddenly
woke up and demanded with one voice:

"Who is this Priam Farll?"

Though the query remained unanswered, Priam
Farll's reputation was henceforward absolutely assured,
and this in spite of the fact that he omitted to comply
with the regulations ordained by English society for
the conduct of successful painters. He ought, first, to
have taken the elementary precaution of being born in
the United States. He ought, after having refused all
interviews for months, to have ultimately granted a
special one to a newspaper with the largest circulation.
He ought to have returned to England, grown a mane
and a tufted tail, and become the king of beasts; or at
least to have made a speech at a banquet about the
noble and purifying mission of art. Assuredly he ought
to have painted the portrait of his father or grandfather
as an artisan, to prove that he was not a snob. But
no! Not content with making each of his pictures utterly different from all the others, he neglected all the
above formalities—and yet managed to pile triumph on
triumph. There are some men of whom it may be
said that, like a punter on a good day, they can't do
wrong. Priam Farll was one such. In a few years he

had become a legend, a standing side-dish of a riddle. No one knew him; no one saw him; no one married him. Constantly abroad, he was ever the subject of conflicting rumours. Parfitts themselves, his London agents, knew naught of him but his handwriting—on the backs of cheques in four figures. They sold an average of five large and five small pictures for him every year. These pictures arrived out of the unknown and the cheques went into the unknown.

Young artists, mute in admiration before the masterpieces from his brush which enriched all the national galleries of Europe (save, of course, that in Trafalgar Square), dreamt of him, worshipped him, and quarrelled fiercely about him, as the very symbol of glory, luxury and flawless accomplishment, never conceiving him as a man like themselves, with boots to lace up, a palette to clean, a beating heart, and an instinctive fear of solitude.

Finally there came to him the paramount distinction, the last proof that he was appreciated. The press actually fell into the habit of mentioning his name without explanatory comment. Exactly as it does not write "Mr. A. J. Balfour, the eminent statesman," or "Sarah Bernhardt, the renowned actress," or "Charles Peace, the historic murderer," but simply "Mr. A. J. Balfour," "Sarah Bernhardt" or "Charles Peace;" so it wrote simply "Mr. Priam Farll." And no occupant of a smoker in a morning train ever took his pipe out of his mouth to ask, "What is the Johnny?" Greater honour in England hath no man. Priam Farll was the first English painter to enjoy this supreme social reward.

And now he was inhabiting the puce dressing-gown.

THE DREADFUL SECRET.

A bell startled the forlorn house; its loud old-fashioned jangle came echoingly up the basement stairs and struck the ear of Priam Farll, who half rose and then sat down again. He knew that it was an urgent summons to the front door, and that none but he could answer it; and yet he hesitated.

Leaving Priam Farll, the great and wealthy artist, we return to that far more interesting person, Priam Farll the private human creature; and come at once to the dreadful secret of his character, the trait in him which explained the peculiar circumstances of his life.

As a private human creature, he happened to be shy.

He was quite different from you or me. We never feel secret qualms at the prospect of meeting strangers, or of taking quarters at a grand hotel, or of entering a large house for the first time, or of walking across a room full of seated people, or of dismissing a servant, or of arguing with a haughty female aristocrat behind a post-office counter, or of passing a shop where we owe money. As for blushing or hanging back, or even looking awkward, when faced with any such simple, everyday acts, the idea of conduct so childish would not occur to us. We behave naturally under all circumstances—for why should a sane man behave otherwise? Priam Farll was different. To call the world's attention visually to the fact of his own existence was anguish to him. But in a letter he could be absolutely brazen. Give him a pen and he was fearless.

Now he knew that he would have to go and open the front door. Both humanity and self-interest urged him to go instantly. For the visitant was assuredly the doctor, come at last to see the sick man lying upstairs. The sick man was Henry Leek, and Henry Leek was Priam Farll's bad habit. While somewhat of a rascal (as his master guessed), Leek was a very perfect valet. Like you and me, he was never shy. He always did the natural thing naturally. He had become, little by little, indispensable to Priam Farll, the sole means of living communication between Priam Farll and the universe of men. The master's shyness, resembling a deer's, kept the pair almost entirely out of England, and, on their continuous travels, the servant invariably stood between that sensitive diffidence and the world. Leek saw everyone who had to be seen, and did every-

2*

thing that involved personal contacts. And, being a bad habit, he had of course grown on Priam Farll, and thus, year after year, for a quarter of a century, Farll's shyness, with his riches and his glory, had increased. Happily Leek was never ill. That is to say, he never had been ill, until this day of their sudden incognito arrival in London for a brief sojourn. He could hardly have chosen a more inconvenient moment; for in London of all places, in that inherited house in Selwood Terrace which he so seldom used, Priam Farll could not carry on daily life without him. It really was unpleasant and disturbing in the highest degree, this illness of Leek's. The fellow had apparently caught cold on the night-boat. He had fought the approaches of insidious disease for several hours, going forth to make purchases and incidentally consulting a doctor; and then, without warning, in the very act of making up Priam Farll's couch, he had abandoned the struggle, and, since his own bed was not ready, he had taken to his master's. He always did the natural thing naturally. And Farll had been forced to help him to undress!

From this point onwards Priam Farll, opulent though he was and illustrious, had sunk to a tragic impotence. He could do nothing for himself; and he could do nothing for Leek, because Leek refused both brandy and sandwiches, and the larder consisted solely of brandy and sandwiches. The man lay upstairs there, comatose, still, silent, waiting for the doctor who had promised to pay an evening visit. And the summer day had darkened into the summer night.

The notion of issuing out into the world and personally obtaining food for himself or aid for Leek, did genuinely seem to Priam Farll an impossible notion; he had never done such things. For him a shop was an impregnable fort garrisoned by ogres. Besides, it would have been necessary to 'ask,' and 'asking' was the torture of tortures. So he had wandered, solicitous and helpless, up and down the stairs, until at length Leek, ceasing to be a valet and deteriorating into a mere human organism, had feebly yet curtly requested to be just let alone, asserting that he was right enough. Whereupon the envied of all painters, the symbol of artistic glory and triumph, had assumed the valet's notorious puce dressing-gown and established himself in a hard chair for a night of discomfort.

The bell rang once more, and there was a sharp impressive knock that reverberated through the forlorn house in a most portentous and terrifying manner. It might have been death knocking. It engendered the horrible suspicion, "Suppose he's *seriously* ill?" Priam Farll sprang up nervously, braced to meet ringers and knockers.

CURE FOR SHYNESS.

On the other side of the door, dressed in frock coat
and silk hat, there stood hesitating a tall, thin, weary
man who had been afoot for exactly twenty hours, in
pursuit of his usual business of curing imaginary
ailments by means of medicine and suggestion, and
leaving real ailments to nature aided by coloured water.
His attitude towards the medical profession was somewhat sardonic, partly because he was convinced that
only the gluttony of South Kensington provided him with
a livelihood, but more because his wife and two fully-
developed daughters spent too much on their frocks.
For years, losing sight of the fact that he was an immortal soul, they had been treating him as a breakfast-
in-the-slot machine: they put a breakfast in the slot,
pushed a button of his waistcoat, and drew out banknotes.   For this, he had neither partner, nor assistant,
nor carriage, nor holiday: his wife and daughters could
not afford him these luxuries.   He was able, con-
scientious, chronically tired, bald and fifty.   He was
also, strange as it may seem, shy; though indeed he
had grown used to it, as a man gets used to a hollow
tooth or an eel to skinning.   No qualities of the young
girl's heart about the heart of Dr. Cashmore!   He really
did know human nature, and he never dreamt of any-

thing more paradisiacal than a Sunday Pullman escapade to Brighton.

Priam Farll opened the door which divided these two hesitating men, and they saw each other by the light of the gas lamp (for the hall was in darkness).

"This Mr. Farll's?" asked Dr. Cashmore, with the unintentional asperity of shyness.

As for Priam, the revelation of his name by Leek shocked him almost into a sweat. Surely the number of the house should have sufficed.

"Yes," he admitted, half shy and half vexed. "Are you the doctor?"

"Yes."

Dr. Cashmore stepped into the obscurity of the hall.

"How's the invalid going on?"

"I can scarcely tell you," said Priam. "He's in bed, very quiet."

"That's right," said the doctor. "When he came to my surgery this morning I advised him to go to bed."

Then followed a brief awkward pause, during which Priam Farll coughed and the doctor rubbed his hands and hummed a fragment of melody.

"By Jove!" the thought flashed through the mind of Farll. "This chap's shy, I do believe!"

And through the mind of the doctor, "Here's another of 'em, all nerves!"

They both instantly, from sheer good-natured con-
descension the one to the other, became at ease. It
was as if a spring had been loosed. Priam shut the
door and shut out the ray of the street lamp.

"I'm afraid there's no light here," said he.

"I'll strike a match," said the doctor.

"Thanks very much," said Priam.

The flare of a wax vesta illumined the splendours
of the puce dressing-gown. But Dr. Cashmore did not
blench. He could flatter himself that in the matter of
dressing-gowns he had nothing to learn.

"By the way, what's wrong with him, do you think?"
Priam Farll inquired in his most boyish voice.

"Don't know. Chill! He had a loud cardiac murmur. Might be anything. That's why I said I'd call
anyhow to-night. Couldn't come any sooner. Been on
my feet since six o'clock this morning. You know what
it is—G. P.'s day."

He smiled grimly in his fatigue.

"It's very good of you to come," said Priam Farll
with warm, vivacious sympathy. He had an astonishing gift for imaginatively putting himself in the place of
other people.

"Not at all!" the doctor muttered. He was quite
touched. To hide the fact that he was touched he
struck a second match. "Shall we go upstairs?"

In the bedroom a candle was burning on a dusty

and empty dressing-table. Dr. Cashmore moved it to the vicinity of the bed, which was like an oasis of decent arrangement in the desert of comfortless chamber; then he stooped to examine the sick valet.

"He's shivering!" exclaimed the doctor softly.

Henry Leek's skin was indeed bluish, though, besides blankets, there was a considerable apparatus of rugs on the bed, and the night was warm. His ageing face (for he was the third man of fifty in that room) had an anxious look. But he made no movement, uttered no word, at sight of the doctor; just stared, dully. His own difficult breathing alone seemed to interest him.

"Any women up?"

The doctor turned suddenly and fiercely on Priam Farll, who started.

"There's only ourselves in the house," he replied.

A person less experienced than Dr. Cashmore in the secret strangenesses of genteel life in London might have been astonished by this information. But Dr. Cashmore no more blenched now than he had blenched at the puce garment.

"Well, hurry up and get some hot water," said he, in a tone dictatorial and savage. "Quick, now! And brandy! And more blankets! Now don't stand there, please! Here! I'll go with you to the kitchen. Show me!" He snatched up the candle, and the expression of his features said, "I can see you're no good in a crisis."

"It's all up with me, doctor," came a faint whisper from the bed.

"So it is, my boy!" said the doctor under his breath as he tumbled downstairs in the wake of Priam Farll. "Unless I get something hot into you!"

MASTER AND SERVANT.

"Will there have to be an inquest?" Priam Farll asked at 6 a.m.

He had collapsed in the hard chair on the ground-floor. The indispensable Henry Leek was lost to him for ever. He could not imagine what would happen to his existence in the future. He could not conceive himself without Leek. And, still worse, the immediate prospect of unknown horrors of publicity in connection with the death of Leek overwhelmed him.

"No!" said the doctor, cheerfully. "Oh no! I was present. Acute double pneumonia! Sometimes happens like that! I can give a certificate. But of course you will have to go to the registrar's and register the death."

Even without an inquest, he saw that the affair would be unthinkably distressing. He felt that it would kill him, and he put his hand to his face.

"Where are Mr. Farll's relatives to be found?" the doctor asked.

"Mr. Farll's relatives?" Priam Farll repeated without comprehending.

Then he understood. Dr. Cashmore thought that Henry Leek's name was Farll! And all the sensitive timidity in Priam Farll's character seized swiftly at the mad chance of escape from any kind of public appearance as Priam Farll. Why should he not let it be supposed that he, and not Henry Leek, had expired suddenly in Selwood Terrace at 5 a.m. He would be free, utterly free!

"Yes," said the doctor. "They must be informed, naturally."

Priam's mind ran rapidly over the catalogue of his family. He could think of no one nearer than a certain Duncan Farll, a second cousin.

"I don't think he had any," he replied in a voice that trembled with excitement at the capricious rashness of what he was doing. "Perhaps there were distant cousins. But Mr. Farll never talked of them."

Which was true.

He could scarcely articulate the words "Mr. Farll." But when they were out of his mouth he felt that the deed was somehow definitely done.

The doctor gazed at Priam's hands, the rough,

coarsened hands of a painter who is always messing in oils and dust.

"Pardon me," said the doctor. "I presume you are his valet—or——"

"Yes," said Priam Farll.

That set the seal.

"What was your master's full name?" the doctor demanded.

And Priam Farll shivered.

"Priam Farll," said he weakly.

"Not *the*——?" loudly exclaimed the doctor, whom the hazards of life in London had at last staggered.

Priam nodded.

"Well, well!" The doctor gave vent to his feelings. The truth was that this particular hazard of life in London pleased him, flattered him, made him feel important in the world, and caused him to forget his fatigue and his wrongs.

He saw that the puce dressing-gown contained a man who was at the end of his tether, and with that good nature of his which no hardships had been able to destroy, he offered to attend to the preliminary formalities. Then he went.

A MONTH'S WAGES.

Priam Farll had no intention of falling asleep; his desire was to consider the position which he had so rashly created for himself; but he did fall asleep—and in the hard chair! He was awakened by a tremendous clatter, as if the house was being bombarded and there were bricks falling about his ears. When he regained all his senses this bombardment resolved itself into nothing but a loud and continued assault on the front-door. He rose, and saw a frowsy, dishevelled, puce-coloured figure in the dirty mirror over the fireplace And then, with stiff limbs, he directed his sleepy feet towards the door.

Dr. Cashmore was at the door, and still another man of fifty, a stern-set, blue-chinned, stoutish person in deep and perfect mourning, including black gloves.

This person gazed coldly at Priam Farll.

"Ah!" ejaculated the mourner.

And stepped in, followed by Dr. Cashmore.

In achieving the inner mat the mourner perceived a white square on the floor. He picked it up and carefully examined it, and then handed it to Priam Farll.

"I suppose this is for you," said he.

Priam, accepting the envelope, saw that it was addressed to "Henry Leek, Esq., 91 Selwood Terrace, S.W.," in a woman's hand.

"It *is* for you, isn't it?" pursued the mourner in an inflexible voice.

"Yes," said Priam.

"I am Mr. Duncan Farll, a solicitor, a cousin of your late employer," the metallic voice continued, coming through a set of large, fine, white teeth. "What arrangements have you made during the day?"

Priam stammered: "None. I've been asleep."

"You aren't very respectful," said Duncan Farll.

So this was his second cousin, whom he had met, once only, as a boy! Never would he have recognised Duncan. Evidently it did not occur to Duncan to recognise him. People are apt to grow unrecognisable in the course of forty years.

Duncan Farll strode about the ground-floor of the house, and on the threshold of each room ejaculated "Ah!" or "Ha!" Then he and the doctor went upstairs. Priam remained inert, and excessively disturbed, in the hall.

At length Duncan Farll descended.

"Come in here, Leek," said Duncan.

And Priam meekly stepped after him into the room where the hard chair was. Duncan Farll took the hard chair.

"What are your wages?"

Priam sought to remember how much he had paid Henry Leek.

"A hundred a year," said he.

"Ah! A good wage. When were you last paid?"

Priam remembered that he had paid Leek two days ago.

"The day before yesterday," said he.

"I must say again you are not very respectful," Duncan observed, drawing forth his pocket-book. "However, here is £8 7s., a month's wages in lieu of notice. Put your things together, and go. I shall have no further use for you. I will make no observations of any kind. But be good enough to *dress*—it is three o'clock—and leave the house at once. Let me see your box or boxes before you go."

When an hour later, in the gloaming, Priam Farll stood on the wrong side of his own door, with Henry Leek's heavy kit-bag and Henry Leek's tin trunk flanking him on either hand, he saw that events in his career were moving with immense rapidity. He had wanted to be free, and free he was. Quite free! But it appeared to him very remarkable that so much could happen, in so short a time, as the result of a mere momentary impulsive prevarication.

CHAPTER II.

A PAIL.

STICKING out of the pocket of Leek's light overcoat was a folded copy of the *Daily Telegraph*. Priam Farll was something of a dandy, and like all right-thinking dandies and all tailors, he objected to the suave line of a garment being spoilt by a free utilisation of pockets. The overcoat itself, and the suit beneath, were quite good; for, though they were the property of the late Henry Leek, they perfectly fitted Priam Farll and had recently belonged to him, Leek having been accustomed to clothe himself entirely from his master's wardrobe. The dandy absently drew forth the *Telegraph,* and the first thing that caught his eye was this: "A beautiful private hotel of the highest class. Luxuriously furnished. Visitor's comfort studied. Finest position in London. Cuisine a speciality. Quiet. Suitable for persons of superior rank. Bathroom. Electric light. Separate tables. No irritating extras. Single rooms from 2½ guineas, double from 4 guineas weekly. 250 Queen's Gate." And below this he saw another piece of news: "Not a boarding-house. A magnificent mansion. Forty bedrooms by Waring. Superb public saloons by Maple. Parisian chef. Separate tables. Four bathrooms. Card-room, billiard-room, vast lounge. Young, cheerful, musical society. Bridge (small). Special sanitation. Finest position in London. No irritating extras. Single rooms from 2½ guineas, double from 4 guineas weekly. Phone 10,073 Western. Trefusis Mansion, W."

At that moment a hansom cab came ambling down Selwood Terrace.

Impulsively he hailed it.

" 'Ere, guv'nor," said the cabman, seeing with an expert eye that Priam Farll was unaccustomed to the manipulation of luggage. "Give this 'ere Hacken-schmidt a copper to lend ye a hand. You're only a light weight."

A small and emaciated boy, with the historic re-mains of a cigarette in his mouth, sprang like a monkey up the steps, and, not waiting to be asked, snatched the trunk from Priam's hands. Priam gave him one of Leek's sixpences for his feats of strength, and the boy spat generously on the coin, at the same time, by a strange skill, clinging to the cigarette with his lower lip. Then the driver lifted the reins with a noble gesture, and Priam had to be decisive and get into the cab.

"250 Queen's Gate," said he.

As, keeping his head to one side to avoid the reins, he gave the direction across the roof of the cab to the attentive cocked ear of the cabman, he felt suddenly that he had regained his nationality, that he was utterly English, in an atmosphere utterly English. The hansom was like home after the wilderness.

He had chosen 250 Queen's Gate because it appeared the abode of tranquillity and discretion. He felt that he might sink into 250 Queen's Gate as into a feather bed. The other palace intimidated him. It recalled the terrors of a continental hotel. In his wanderings he had suffered much from the young, cheerful and musical society of bright hotels, and bridge (small) had no attraction for him.

As the cab tinkled through canyons of familiar stucco, he looked further at the *Telegraph*. He was rather surprised to find more than a column of enticing palaces, each in the finest position in London; London, in fact, seemed to be one unique, glorious position. And it was so welcome, so receptive, so wishful to make a speciality of your comfort, your food, your bath, your sanitation! He remembered the old boarding-houses of the eighties. Now all was changed, for the better. The *Telegraph* was full of the better, crammed and packed with tight columns of it. The better burst aspiringly from the tops of columns on the first page and outsoared the very title of the paper. He saw there, for instance, to the left of the title, a new, refined tea-house in Piccadilly Circus, owned and managed by gentlewomen, where you had real tea and real bread-and-butter and real cakes in a real drawing-room. It was astounding.

The cab stopped.

"Is this it?" he asked the driver.

"This is 250, sir."

And it was. But it did not resemble even a private hotel. It exactly resembled a private house, narrow and tall and squeezed in between its sister and its brother. Priam Farll was puzzled, till the solution occurred to him. "Of course," he said to himself. "This is the quietude, the discretion. I shall like this." He jumped down.

"I'll keep you," he threw to the cabman, in the proper phrase (which he was proud to recall from his youth), as though the cabman had been something which he had ordered on approval.

There were two bell-knobs. He pulled one, and waited for the portals to open on discreet vistas of luxurious furniture. No response! Then he pulled the other knob. Still no response! Just as he was consulting the *Telegraph* to make sure of the number, the door silently swung back, and disclosed the figure of a middle-aged woman in black silk, who regarded him with a stern astonishment.

"Is this——?" he began, nervous and abashed by her formidable stare.

3*

"Were you wanting rooms?" she asked.

"Yes," said he. "I was. If I could just see——"

"Will you come in?" she said. And her morose face, under stringent commands from her brain, began an imitation of a smile which, as an imitation, was wonderful. It made you wonder how she had ever taught her face to do it.

Priam Farll found himself blushing on a Turkey carpet, and a sort of cathedral gloom around him. He was disconcerted, but the Turkey carpet assured him somewhat. As his eyes grew habituated to the light he saw that the cathedral was very narrow, and that instead of the choir was a staircase, also clothed in Turkey carpet. On the lowest step reposed an object whose nature he could not at first determine.

"Would it be for long?" the lips opposite him muttered cautiously.

His reply—the reply of an impulsive, shy nature—was to rush out of the palace. He had identified the object on the stairs. It was a slop-pail with a wrung cloth on its head.

He felt profoundly discouraged and pessimistic. All his energy had left him. London had become hard, hostile, cruel, impossible. He longed for Leek with a great longing.

TEA.

An hour later, having at the kind suggestion of the cabman deposited Leek's goods at the cloak-room of South Kensington Station, he was wandering on foot out of old London into the central ring of new London, where people never do anything except take the air in parks, lounge in club-windows, roll to and fro in peculiar vehicles that have ventured out without horses and are making the best of it, buy flowers and Egyptian cigarettes, look at pictures, and eat and drink. Nearly all the buildings were higher than they used to be, and the street wider; and at intervals of a hundred yards or so cranes that rent the clouds and defied the law of gravity were continually swinging bricks and marble into the upper layers of the air. Violets were on sale at every corner, and the atmosphere was impregnated with an intoxicating perfume of methylated spirits. Presently he arrived at an immense arched façade bearing principally the legend "Tea," and he saw within hundreds of persons sipping tea; and next to that was another arched façade bearing principally the word "Tea," and he saw within more hundreds sipping tea; and then another; and then another; and then suddenly he came to an open circular place that seemed vaguely familiar.

"By Jove!" he said. "This is Piccadilly Circus!"

And just at that moment, over a narrow doorway,
he perceived the image of a green tree, and the words,
"The Elm Tree." It was the entrance to the Elm Tree
Tea Rooms, so well spoken of in the *Telegraph*. In
certain ways he was a man of advanced and humane
ideas, and the thought of delicately nurtured needy
gentlewomen bravely battling with the world instead of
starving as they used to starve in the past, appealed to
his chivalry. He determined to assist them by taking
tea in the advertised drawing-room. Gathering together
his courage, he penetrated into a corridor lighted by
pink electricity, and then up pink stairs. A pink door
stopped him at last. It might have hid mysterious and
questionable things, but it said laconically "Push," and
he courageously pushed. . . . He was in a kind of
boudoir thickly populated with tables and chairs. The
swift transmigration from the blatant street to a drawing-
room had a startling effect on him: it caused him to
whip off his hat as though his hat had been red hot.
Except for two tall elegant creatures who stood together
at the other end of the boudoir, the chairs and tables
had the place to themselves. He was about to stammer
an excuse and fly, when one of the gentlewomen turned
her eye on him for a moment, and so he sat down.
The gentlewomen then resumed their conversation. He
glanced cautiously about him. Elm-trees, firmly rooted
in a border of Indian matting, grew round all the walls

in exotic profusion, and their topmost branches splashed over onto the ceiling. A card on the trunk of a tree, announcing curtly, "Dogs not allowed," seemed to enhearten him. After a pause one of the gentlewomen swam haughtily towards him and looked him between the eyes. She spoke no word, but her firm, austere glance said:

"Now, out with it, and see you behave yourself!"

He had been ready to smile chivalrously. But the smile was put to sudden death.

"Some tea, please," he said faintly, and his intimidated tone said, "If it isn't troubling you too much."

"What do you want with it?" asked the gentlewoman abruptly, and as he was plainly at a loss she added, "Crumpets or tea-cake?"

"Tea-cake," he replied, though he hated tea-cake. But he was afraid.

"You've escaped this time," said the drapery of her muslins as she swam from his sight. "But no nonsense while I'm away!"

When she sternly and mutely thrust the refection before him, he found that everything on the table except the tea-cakes and the spoon was growing elm-trees.

After one cup and one slice, when the tea had become stewed and undrinkable, and the tea-cake a material suitable for the manufacture of shooting boots, he resumed, at any rate partially, his presence of mind, and remembered that he had done nothing positively criminal in entering the boudoir or drawing-room and requesting food in return for money. Besides, the gentlewomen were now pretending to each other that he did not exist, and no other rash persons had been driven by hunger into the virgin forest of elm-trees. He began to meditate, and his meditations, taking—for him—an unusual turn, caused him surreptitiously to examine Henry Leek's pocket-book (previously only known to him by sight). He had not for many years troubled himself concerning money, but the discovery that, when he had paid for the deposit of luggage at the cloak-room, a solitary sovereign rested in the pocket of Leek's trousers, had suggested to him that it would be advisable sooner or later to consider the financial aspect of existence.

There were two banknotes for ten pounds each in Leek's pocket-book; also five French banknotes of a thousand francs each, and a number of Italian banknotes of small denominations: the equivalent of two hundred and thirty pounds altogether, not counting a folded inch-rule, some postage stamps, and a photograph of a pleasant-faced woman of forty or so. This sum seemed neither vast nor insignificant to Priam Farll. It seemed to him merely a tangible something which would enable him to banish the fiscal question from his mind for an indefinite period. He scarcely even troubled to wonder what Leek was doing with over two years of Leek's income in his pocket-book. He knew, or at least he with certainty guessed, that Leek had been a rascal. Still, he had had a sort of grim, cynical affection for Leek. And the thought that Leek would never again shave him, nor tell him in accents that brooked no delay that his hair must be cut, nor register his luggage and secure his seat on long-distance expresses, filled him with very real melancholy. He did not feel sorry for Leek, nor say to himself "Poor Leek!" Nobody who had had the advantage of Leek's acquaintance would have said "Poor Leek!" For Leek's greatest speciality had always been the speciality of looking after Leek, and wherever Leek might be it was a surety that Leek's interests would not suffer. Therefore Priam Farll's pity was mainly self-centred.

And though his dignity had been considerably damaged during the final moments at Selwood Terrace, there was matter for congratulation. The doctor, for instance, had shaken hands with him at parting; had shaken hands openly, in the presence of Duncan Farll: a flattering tribute to his personality. But the chief of Priam Farll's satisfactions in that desolate hour was that he had suppressed himself, that for the world he existed no more. I shall admit frankly that this satisfaction nearly outweighed his grief. He sighed—and it was a sigh of tremendous relief. For now, by a miracle, he would be free from the menace of Lady Sophia Entwistle. Looking back in calmness at the still recent Entwistle episode in Paris—the real originating cause of his sudden flight to London—he was staggered by his latent capacity for downright, impulsive foolishness. Like all shy people he had fits of amazing audacity—and his recklessness usually took the form of making himself agreeable to women whom he encountered in travel (he was much less shy with women than with men). But to propose marriage to a weather-beaten haunter of hotels like Lady Sophia Entwistle, and to reveal his identity to her, and to allow her to accept his proposal—the thing had been unimaginably inept!

And now he was free, for he was dead.

He was conscious of a chill in the spine as he dwelt on the awful fate which he had escaped. He, a man of fifty, a man of set habits, a man habituated to the liberty of the wild stag, to bow his proud neck under the solid footwear of Lady Sophia Entwistle!

Yes, there was most decidedly a silver lining to the dark cloud of Leek's translation to another sphere of activity.

In replacing the pocket-book his hand encountered the letter which had arrived for Leek in the morning. Arguing with himself whether he ought to open it, he opened it. It ran: "Dear Mr. Leek, I am so glad to have your letter, and I think the photograph is most gentlemanly. But I do wish you would not write with a type-writer. You don't know how this affects a woman, or you wouldn't do it. However, I shall be so glad to meet you now, as you suggest. Suppose we go to Maskelyne and Cook's together to-morrow afternoon (Saturday). You know it isn't the Egyptian Hall any more. It is in St. George's Hall, I think. But you will see it in the *Telegraph;* also the time. I will be there when the doors open. You will recognise me from my photograph; but I shall wear red roses in my hat. So *au revoir* for the present. Yours sincerely, Alice Challice. P.S.—There are always a lot of dark parts at Maskelyne and Cook's. I must ask you to behave as a gentleman should. Excuse me. I merely mention it in case.—A. C."

Infamous Leek! Here was at any rate one explanation of a mysterious little type-writer which the valet had always carried, but which Priam had left at Selwood Terrace.

Priam glanced at the photograph in the pocketbook; and also, strange to say, at the *Telegraph*.

A lady with three children burst into the drawing-room, and instantly occupied the whole of it; the children cried "Mathaw!" "Mathah!" "Mathaw!" in shrill tones of varied joy. As one of the gentlewomen passed near him, he asked modestly—

"How much, please?"

She dropped a flake of paper onto his table without arresting her course, and said warningly:

"You pay at the desk."

When he hit on the desk, which was hidden behind a screen of elm-trees, he had to face a true aristocrat— and not in muslins, either. If the others were the daughters of earls, this was the authentic countess in a tea-gown.

He put down Leek's sovereign.

"Haven't you anything smaller?" snapped the countess.

"I'm sorry I haven't," he replied.

She picked up the sovereign scornfully, and turned it over.

"It's very awkward," she muttered.

Then she unlocked two drawers, and unwillingly gave him eighteen and sixpence in silver and copper, without another word and without looking at him.

"Thank you," said he, pocketing it nervously.

And, amid reiterated cries of "Mathah!" "Mathaw!" "Mathah!" he hurried away, unregarded, unregretted, splendidly repudiated by these delicate refined creatures who were struggling for a livelihood in a great city.

ALICE CHALLICE.

"I suppose you are Mr. Leek, aren't you?" a woman greeted him as he stood vaguely hesitant outside St. George's Hall, watching the afternoon audience emerge. He started back, as though the woman with her trace of Cockney accent had presented a revolver at his head. He was very much afraid. It may reasonably be asked what he was doing up at St. George's Hall. The answer to this most natural question touches the deepest springs of human conduct. There were two men in Priam Farll. One was the shy man, who had long ago persuaded himself that he actually preferred not to mix with his kind, and had made a virtue of his cowardice. The other was a doggish, devil-may-care fellow who loved dashing adventures and had a perfect passion for free intercourse with the entire human race. No. 2 would often lead No. 1 unsuspectingly forward to a difficult situation from which No. 1, though angry and uncomfortable, could not retire.

Thus it was No. 2 who with the most casual air had wandered up Regent Street, drawn by the slender chance of meeting a woman with red roses in her hat; and it was No. 1 who had to pay the penalty. Nobody could have been more astonished than No. 2 at the fulfilment of No. 2's secret yearning for novelty. But the

innocent sincerity of No. 2's astonishment gave no aid to
No. 1.

Farll raised his hat, and at the same moment perceived the roses. He might have denied the name of
Leek and fled, but he did not. Though his left leg was
ready to run, his right leg would not stir.

Then he was shaking hands with her. But how
had she identified him?

"I didn't really expect you," said the lady, always
with a slight Cockney accent. "But I thought how silly
it would be for me to miss the vanishing trick just because you couldn't come. So in I went, by myself."

"Why didn't you expect me?" he asked diffidently.

"Well," she said, "Mr. Farll being dead, I knew
you'd have a lot to do, besides being upset like."

"Oh yes," he said quickly, feeling that he must be
more careful; for he had quite forgotten that Mr. Farll
was dead. "How did you know?"

"How did I know!" she cried. "Well, I like that!
Look anywhere! It's all over London, has been these
six hours." She pointed to a ragged man who was
wearing an orange-coloured placard by way of apron.
On the placard was printed in large black letters:
"Sudden death of Priam Farll in London. Special
Memoir." Other ragged men, also wearing aprons, but
of different colours, similarly proclaimed by their attire
that Priam Farll was dead. And people crowding out

of St. George's Hall were continually buying newspapers from these middlemen of tidings.

He blushed. It was singular that he could have walked even half-an-hour in Central London without noticing that his own name flew in the summer breeze of every street. But so it had been. He was that sort of man. Now he understood how Duncan Farll had descended upon Selwood Terrace.

"You don't mean to say you didn't *see* those posters?" she demanded.

"I didn't," he said simply.

"That shows how you must have been thinking!" said she. "Was he a good master?"

"Yes, very good," said Priam Farll with conviction.

"I see you're not in mourning."

"No. That is——"

"I don't hold with mourning myself," she proceeded. "They say it's to show respect. But it seems to me that if you can't show your respect without a pair of black gloves that the dye's always coming off . . . I don't know what you think, but I never did hold with mourning. It's grumbling against Providence too! Not but what I think there's a good deal too much talk about Providence. I don't know what you think, but——"

"I quite agree with you," he said, with a warm generous smile which sometimes rushed up and trans-

formed his face before he was aware of the occurrence.

And she smiled also, gazing at him half confidentially. She was a little woman, stoutish—indeed,
stout; puffy red cheeks; a too remarkable white cotton
blouse; and a crimson skirt that hung unevenly; grey
cotton gloves; a green sunshade; on the top of all this
the black hat with red roses. The photograph in Leek's
pocket-book must have been taken in the past. She
looked quite forty-five, whereas the photograph indicated thirty-nine and a fraction. He gazed down at
her protectively, with a good-natured appreciative con-
descension.

"I suppose you'll have to be going back again
soon, to arrange things like," she said. It was always
she who kept the conversation afloat.

"No," he said. "I've finished there. They've dismissed me."

"Who have?"

"The relatives."

"Why?"

He shook his head.

"I hope you made them pay you your month," said
she firmly.

He was glad to be able to give a satisfactory answer.

After a pause she resumed bravely:

"So Mr. Farll was one of these artists? At least so I see according to the paper."

He nodded.

"It's a very funny business," she said. "But I suppose there's some of them make quite a nice income out of it. *You* ought to know about that, being in it, as it were."

Never in his life had he conversed on such terms with such a person as Mrs. Alice Challice. She was in every way a novelty for him—in clothes, manners, accent, deportment, outlook on the world and on paint. He had heard and read of such beings as Mrs. Alice Challice, and now he was in direct contact with one of them. The whole affair struck him as excessively odd, as a mad escapade on his part. Wisdom in him deemed it ridiculous to prolong the encounter, but shy folly could not break loose. Moreover she possessed the charm of her novelty; and there was that in her which challenged the male in him.

"Well," she said, "I suppose we can't stand here for ever!"

The crowd had frittered itself away, and an attendant was closing and locking the doors of St. George's Hall. He coughed.

"It's a pity it's Saturday and all the shops closed. But anyhow suppose we walk along Oxford Street all the same? Shall we?" This from her.

"By all means."

"Now there's one thing I should like to say," she murmured with a calm smile as they moved off. "You've no occasion to be shy with me. There's no call for it. I'm just as you see me."

"Shy!" he exclaimed, genuinely surprised. "Do I seem shy to you?" He thought he had been magnificently doggish.

"Oh, well," she said. "That's all right, then, if you *aren't*. I should take it as a poor compliment, being shy with me. Where do you think we can have a good talk? I'm free for the evening. I don't know about you."

Her eyes questioned his.

NO GRATUITIES.

At a later hour, they were entering, side by side, a glittering establishment whose interior seemed to be walled chiefly in bevelled glass, so that everywhere the curious observer saw himself and twisted fractions of himself. The glass was relieved at frequent intervals by elaborate enamelled signs which repeated, "No gratuities." It seemed that the directors of the establishment wished to make perfectly clear to visitors that, whatever else they might find, they must on no account expect gratuities.

"I've always wanted to come here," said Mrs. Alice Challice vivaciously, glancing up at Priam Farll's modest, middle-aged face.

Then, after they had successfully passed through a preliminary pair of bevelled portals, a huge man dressed like a policeman, and achieving a very successful imitation of a policeman, stretched out his hand, and stopped them.

"In line, please," he said.

"I thought it was a restaurant, not a theatre," Priam whispered to Mrs. Challice.

"So it is a restaurant," said his companion. "But I hear they're obliged to do like this because there's always such a crowd. It's very 'andsome, isn't it?"

He agreed that it was. He felt that London had got a long way in front of him and that he would have to hurry a great deal before he could catch it up.

At length another imitation of a policeman opened more doors and, with other sinners, they were released from purgatory into a clattering paradise, which again offered everything save gratuities. They were conducted to a small table full of dirty plates and empty glasses in a corner of the vast and lofty saloon. A man in evening dress whose eye said, "Now mind, no insulting gratuities!" rushed past the table and in one deft amazing gesture swept off the whole of its contents and was gone with them. It was an astounding feat, and when

Priam recovered from his amazement he fell into another amazement on discovering that by some magic
means the man in evening dress had insinuated a gold-
charactered menu into his hands.   This menu was exceedingly long—it comprised everything except gratuities—and, evidently knowing from experience that it
was not a document to be perused and exhausted in
five minutes, the man in evening dress took care not
to interrupt the studies of Priam Farll and Alice Challice during a full quarter of an hour.   Then he returned like a bolt, put them through an examination
in the menu, and fled, and when he was gone they
saw that the table was set with a clean cloth and in-
struments and empty glasses.   A band thereupon burst
into gay strains, like the band at a music-hall after
something very difficult on the horizontal bar.   And it
played louder and louder; and as it played louder, so
the people talked louder.   And the crash of cymbals
mingled with the crash of plates, and the altercations
of knives and forks with the shrill accents of chatterers
determined to be heard.   And men in evening dress (a
costume which seemed to be forbidden to sitters at
tables) flitted to and fro with inconceivable rapidity,
austere, preoccupied conjurers.   And from every marble
wall, bevelled mirror, and Doric column, there spoke
silently but insistently the haunting legend, "No gratuities."

Thus Priam Farll began his first public meal in modern London. He knew the hotels; he knew the restaurants, of half-a-dozen countries, but he had never been so overwhelmed as he was here. Remembering London as a city of wooden chop-houses, he could scarcely eat for the thoughts that surged through his brain.

"Isn't it amusing?" said Mrs. Challice benignantly, over a glass of lager. "I'm so glad you brought me here. I've always wanted to come."

And then, a few minutes afterwards, she was saying, against the immense din—

"You know, I've been thinking for years of getting married again. And if you really *are* thinking of getting married, what are you to do? You may sit in a chair and wait till eggs are sixpence a dozen, and you'll be no nearer. You must do something. And what is there except a matrimonial agency? I say—what's the matter with a matrimonial agency, anyhow? If you want to get married, you want to get married, and it's no use pretending you don't. I do hate pretending, I do. No shame in wanting to get married, is there? I think a matrimonial agency is a very good, useful thing. They say you're swindled. Well, those that are deserve to be. You can be swindled without a matrimonial agency, seems to me. Not that I've ever been. Plain commonsense people never are. No, if you ask me, matrimonial agencies are the most sensible things—after dress-shields—that's ever been invented.   And I'm sure if anything comes of this, I shall pay the fees with the greatest pleasure.   Now don't you agree with me?"

The whole mystery stood explained.

"Absolutely!" he said.

And felt the skin creeping in the small of his back.

CHAPTER III.

THE PHOTOGRAPH.

FROM the moment of Mrs. Challice's remarks in favour of matrimonial agencies Priam Farll's existence became a torture to him. She was what he had always been accustomed to think of as "a very decent woman;" but really . . .! The sentence is not finished because Priam never finished it in his own mind. Fifty times he conducted the sentence as far as 'really,' and there it dissolved into an uncomfortable cloud.

"I suppose we shall have to be going," said she, when her ice had been eaten and his had melted.

"Yes," said he, and added to himself, "But where?"

However, it would be a relief to get out of the restaurant, and he called for the bill.

While they were waiting for the bill the situation grew more strained. Priam was aware of a desire to fling down sovereigns on the table and rush wildly away. Even Mrs. Challice, vaguely feeling this, had a difficulty in conversing.

"You *are* like your photograph!" she remarked, glancing at his face, which—it should be said—had very much changed within half-an-hour. He had a face capable of a hundred expressions per day. His present expression was one of his anxious expressions, medium in degree. It can be figured in the mask of a person who is locked up in an iron strong-room, and, feeling ill at ease, notices that the walls are getting red-hot at the corners.

"Like my photograph?" he exclaimed, astonished that he should resemble Leek's photograph.

"Yes," she asseverated stoutly. "I knew you at once. Especially by the nose."

"Have you got it here?" he asked, interested to see what portrait of Leek had a nose like his own.

And she pulled out of her handbag a photograph, not of Leek, but of Priam Farll. It was an unmounted print of a negative which he and Leek had taken together for the purposes of a pose in a picture, and it had decidedly a distinguished appearance. But why should Leek despatch photographs of his master to strange ladies introduced through a matrimonial agency? Priam Farll could not imagine—unless it was from sheer unscrupulous, careless bounce.

She gazed at the portrait with obvious joy.

"Now, candidly, don't *you* think it's very, very good?" she demanded.

"I suppose it is," he agreed. He would probably have given two hundred pounds for the courage to ex-

plain to her in a few well-chosen words that there had
been a vast mistake, a huge impulsive indiscretion. But
two hundred thousand pounds would not have bought
that courage.

"I love it," she ejaculated fervently—with heat, and
yet so nicely! And she returned the photograph to her
little bag.

She lowered her voice.

"You haven't told me whether you were ever married.
I've been waiting for that."

He blushed. She was disconcertingly personal.

"No," he said.

"And you've always lived like that, alone like; no
home; travelling about; no one to look after you,
properly?" There was distress in her voice.

He nodded. "One gets accustomed to it."

"Oh yes," she said. "I can understand that."

"No responsibilities," he added.

"No. I can understand all that." Then she
hesitated. "But I do feel so sorry for you . . . all these
years!"

And her eyes were moist, and her tone was so
sincere that Priam Farll found it quite remarkably
affecting. Of course she was talking about Henry Leek,
the humble valet, and not about Leek's illustrious
master. But Priam saw no difference between his lot
and that of Leek. He felt that there was no essential

difference, and that, despite Leek's multiple perfections
as a valet, he never had been looked after—properly.
Her voice made him feel just as sorry for himself as
she was sorry for him; it made him feel that she had a
kind heart, and that a kind heart was the only thing
on earth that really mattered. Ah! If Lady Sophia
Entwistle had spoken to him in such accents . . .!

The bill came. It was so small that he was ashamed
to pay it. The suppression of gratuities enabled the
monarch of this bevelled palace to offer a complete
dinner for about the same price as a thimbleful of tea
and ten drachms of cake a few yards away. Happily
the monarch, foreseeing his shame, had arranged a
peculiar method of payment through a little hole, where
the receiver could see nothing but his blushing hands.
As for the conjurers in evening dress, they apparently
never soiled themselves by contact with specie.

Outside on the pavement, he was at a loss what to
do. You see, he was entirely unfamiliar with Mrs.
Challice's code of etiquette.

"Would you care to go to the Alhambra or somewhere?" he suggested, having a notion that this was the
correct thing to say to a lady whose presence near you
was directly due to her desire for marriage.

"It's very good of you," said she. "But I'm sure
you only say it out of kindness—because you're a
gentleman. It wouldn't be quite nice for you to go to a

music-hall to-night. I know I said I was free for the evening, but I wasn't thinking. It wasn't a hint—no, truly! I think I shall go home—and perhaps some other——"

"I shall see you home," said he quickly. Impulsive, again!

"Would you really like to? Can you?" In the bluish glare of an electricity that made the street whiter than day, she blushed. Yes, she blushed like a girl.

She led him up a side-street where was a kind of railway station unfamiliar to Priam Farll's experience, tiled like a butcher's shop and as clean as Holland. Under her direction he took tickets for a station whose name he had never heard of, and then they passed through steel railings which clacked behind them into a sort of safe deposit, from which the only emergence was a long dim tunnel. Painted hands, pointing to the mysterious word "lifts," waved you onwards down this tunnel. "Hurry up, please," came a voice out of the spectral gloom. Mrs. Challice thereupon ran. Now up the tunnel, opposing all human progress, there blew a steady trade-wind of tremendous force. Immediately Priam began to run the trade-wind removed his hat, which sailed buoyantly back towards the street. He was after it like a youth of twenty, and he recaptured it. But when he reached the extremity of the tunnel

his amazed eyes saw nothing but a great cage of human
animals pressed tightly together behind bars.   There
was a click, and the whole cage sank from his sight into
the earth.

He felt that there was more than he had dreamt of
in the city of miracles.   In a couple of minutes another
cage rose into the tunnel at a different point, vomited
its captives and descended swiftly again with Priam and
many others, and threw him and the rest out into a
white mine consisting of numberless galleries.   He ran
about these interminable galleries underneath London,
at the bidding of painted hands, for a considerable
time, and occasionally magic trains without engines
swept across his vision.   But he could not find even the
spirit of Mrs. Alice Challice in this nether world.

THE NEST.

On letter-paper headed "Grand Babylon Hotel,
London," he was writing in a disguised backward hand,
a note to the following effect: "Duncan Farll, Esq. Sir,
—If any letters or telegrams arrive for me at Selwood
Terrace, be good enough to have them forwarded to
me at once to the above address. — Yours truly,
H. Leek."   It cost him something to sign the name of
the dead man; but he instinctively guessed that Dun-

can Farll might be a sieve which (owing to its legal-
mindedness) would easily get clogged up even by a
slight suspicion. Hence, in order to be sure of receiving a possible letter or telegram from Mrs. Challice, he
must openly label himself as Henry Leek. He had lost
Mrs. Challice; there was no address on her letter; he
only knew that she lived at or near Putney, and the
sole hope of finding her again lay in the fact that she
had the Selwood Terrace address. He wanted to find
her again; he desired that ardently, if merely to explain
to her that their separation was due to a sudden
caprice of his hat, and that he had searched for her
everywhere in the mine, anxiously, desperately. She
would surely not imagine that he had slipped away
from her on purpose? No! And yet, if incapable of
such an enormity, why had she not waited for him on
one of the platforms? However, he hoped for the best.
The best was a telegram; the second-best a letter. On
receipt of which he would fly to her to explain. . . .
And besides, he wanted to see her—simply. Her answer to his suggestion of a music-hall, and the tone of
it, had impressed him. And her remark, "I do feel so
sorry for you all these years," had—well, somewhat
changed his whole outlook on life. Yes, he wanted to
see her in order to satisfy himself that he had her respect. A woman impossible socially, a woman with
strange habits and tricks of manner (no doubt there

were millions such); but a woman whose respect one would not forfeit without a struggle!

He had been pushed to an extremity, forced to act with swiftness, upon losing her. And he had done the thing that comes most naturally to a life-long traveller. He had driven to the best hotel in the town. (He had seen in a flash that the idea of inhabiting any private hotel whatever was a silly idea.) And now he was in a large bedroom overlooking the Thames—a chamber with a writing-desk, a sofa, five electric lights, two easy-chairs, a telephone, electric bells, and a massive oak door with a lock and a key in the lock; in short, his castle! An enterprise of some daring to storm the castle: but he had stormed it. He had registered under the name of Leek, a name sufficiently common not to excite remark, and the floor-valet had proved to be an admirable young man. He trusted to the floor-valet and to the telephone for avoiding any rough contact with the world. He felt comparatively safe now; the entire enormous hotel was a nest for his shyness, a conspiracy to keep him in cotton-wool. He was an autocratic number, absolute ruler over Room 331, and with the right to command the almost limitless resources of the Grand Babylon for his own private ends.

As he sealed the envelope he touched a bell.

The valet entered.

"You've got the evening papers?" asked Priam Farll.

"Yes, sir." The valet put a pile of papers respect-fully on the desk.

"All of them?"

"Yes, sir."

"Thanks. Well, it's not too late to have a mes-senger, is it?"

"Oh *no,* sir." ("'Too late' in the Grand Babylon, oh Czar!" said the valet's shocked tone.)

"Then please get a messenger to take this letter, at once."

"In a cab, sir?"

"Yes, in a cab. I don't know whether there will be an answer. He will see. Then let him call at the cloak-room at South Kensington Station and get my luggage. Here's the ticket."

"Thank you, sir."

"I can rely on you to see that he goes at once?"

"You can, sir," said the valet, in such accents as carry absolute conviction.

"Thank you. That will do, I think."

The man retired, and the door was closed by an expert in closing doors, one who had devoted his life to the perfection of detail in valetry.

FAME.

He lay on the sofa at the foot of the bed, with all illumination extinguished save one crimson-shaded light immediately above him. The evening papers—white, green, rose, cream, and yellow—shared his couch. He was about to glance at the obituaries; to glance at them in a careless, condescending way, just to see the *sort* of thing that journalists had written of him. He knew the value of obituaries; he had often smiled at them. He knew also the exceeding fatuity of art criticism, which did not cause him even to smile, being simply a bore. He recollected, further, that he was not the first man to read his own obituary; the adventure had happened to others; and he could recall how, on his having heard that owing to an error it had happened to the great so-and-so, he, in his quality of philosopher, had instantly decided what frame of mind the great so-and-so ought to have assumed for the perusal of his biography. He carefully and deliberately adopted that frame of mind now. He thought of Marcus Aurelius on the futility of fame; he remembered his life-long attitude of gentle, tired scorn for the press; he reflected with wise modesty that in art nothing counts but the work itself, and that no quantity of inept chatter could possibly affect, for good or evil, his value, such as it might be, to the world.

Then he began to open the papers.

The first glimpse of their contents made him jump. In fact, the physical result of it was quite extraordinary. His temperature increased. His heart became audible. His pulse quickened. And there was a tingling as far off as his toes. He had felt, in a dim, unacknowledged way, that he must be a pretty great painter. Of course his prices were notorious. And he had guessed, though vaguely, that he was the object of widespread curiosity. But he had never compared himself with Titanic figures on the planet. It had always seemed to him that *his* renown was different from other renowns, less—somehow unreal and make-believe. He had never imaginatively grasped, despite prices and public inquisitiveness, that he too was one of the Titanic figures. He grasped it now. The aspect of the papers brought it home to him with tremendous force.

Special large type! Titles stretching across two columns! Black borders round the pages! "Death of England's greatest painter." "Sudden death of Priam Farll." "Sad death of a great genius." "Puzzling career prematurely closed." "Europe is mourning." "Irreparable loss to the world's art." "It is with the most profound regret." "Our readers will be shocked." "The news will come as a personal blow to every lover of great painting." So the papers went on, outvying each other in enthusiastic grief.

He ceased to be careless and condescending to them. The skin crept along his spine. There he lay, solitary, under the crimson glow, locked in his castle, human, with the outward semblance of a man like other men, and yet the cities of Europe were weeping for him. He heard them weeping. Every lover of great painting was under a sense of personal bereavement. The very voice of the world was hushed. After all, it was something to have done your best; after all, good stuff *was* appreciated by the mass of the race. The phenomena presented by the evening papers was certainly prodigious, and prodigiously affecting. Mankind was unpleasantly stunned by the report of his decease. He forgot that Mrs. Challice, for instance, had perfectly succeeded in hiding her grief for the irreparable loss, and that her questions about Priam Farll had been almost perfunctory. He forgot that he had witnessed absolutely no sign of overwhelming sorrow, or of any degree of sorrow, in the thoroughfares of the teeming capital, and that the hotels did not resound to sobbing. He knew only that all Europe was in mourning!

"I suppose I was rather wonderful—*am*, I mean"— he said to himself, dazed and happy. Yes, happy. "The fact is, I've got so used to my own work that perhaps I don't think enough of it." He said this as modestly as he could.

There was no question now of casually glancing at the obituaries. He could not miss a single line, a single word. He even regretted that the details of his life were so few and unimportant. It seemed to him that it was the business of the journalists to have known more, to have displayed more enterprise in acquiring information. Still, the tone was right. The fellows meant well, at any rate. His eyes encountered nothing but praise. Indeed the press of London had yielded itself up to an encomiastic orgy. His modesty tried to say that this was slightly overdone; but his impartiality asked, "Really, what *could* they say against me?" As a rule unmitigated praise was nauseous, but here they were undoubtedly genuine, the fellows; their sentences rang true!

Never in his life had he been so satisfied with the scheme of the universe! He was nearly consoled for the dissolution of Leek.

When, after continued reading, he came across a phrase which discreetly insinuated, apropos of the policeman and the penguins, that capriciousness in the choice of subject was perhaps a pose with him, the accusation hurt.

"Pose!" he inwardly exclaimed. "What a lie! The man's an ass!"

And he resented the following remark which concluded a "special memoir" extremely laudatory in matter and manner, by an expert whose books he had always respected: "However, contemporary judgments are in the large majority of cases notoriously wrong, and it behoves us to remember this in choosing a niche for our idol. Time alone can settle the ultimate position of Priam Farll."

Useless for his modesty to whisper to him that contemporary judgments *were* notoriously wrong. He did not like it. It disturbed him. There were exceptions to every rule. And if the connoisseur meant anything at all, he was simply stultifying the rest of the article. Time be d——d!

He had come nearly to the last line of the last obituary before he was finally ruffled. Most of the sheets, in excusing the paucity of biographical detail, had remarked that Priam Farll was utterly unknown to London society, of a retiring disposition, hating publicity, a recluse, etc. The word "recluse" grated on his sensitiveness a little; but when the least important of the evening papers roundly asserted it to be notorious that he was of extremely eccentric habits, he grew secretly furious. Neither his modesty nor his philosophy was influential enough to restore him to complete calm.

Eccentric! He! What next? Eccentric, indeed!

Now, what conceivable justification——?

THE RULING CLASSES.

Between a quarter-past and half-past eleven he was seated alone at a small table in the restaurant of the Grand Babylon. He had had no news of Mrs. Challice; she had not instantly telegraphed to Selwood Terrace, as he had wildly hoped. But in the boxes of Henry Leek, safely retrieved by the messenger from South Kensington Station, he had discovered one of his old dress-suits, not too old, and this dress-suit he had donned. The desire to move about unknown in the well-clad world, the world of the frequenters of costly hotels, the world to which he was accustomed, had overtaken him. Moreover, he felt hungry. Hence he had descended to the famous restaurant, whose wide windows were flung open to the illuminated majesty of the Thames Embankment. The pale cream room was nearly full of expensive women, and expending men, and silver-chained waiters whose skilled, noiseless, inhuman attentions were remunerated at the rate of about fourpence a minute. Music, the midnight food of love, floated scarce heard through the tinted atmosphere. It was the best imitation of Roman luxury that London could offer, and after Selwood Terrace and the rackety palace of no gratuities, Priam Farll enjoyed it as one enjoys home after strange climes.

Next to his table was an empty table, set for two, to which were presently conducted, with due state, a young man, and a magnificent woman whose youth was slipping off her polished shoulders like a cloak. Priam Farll then overheard the following conversation:—

MAN. Well, what are you going to have?

WOMAN. But look here, little Charlie, you can't possibly afford to pay for this!

MAN. Never said I could. It's the paper that pays. So go ahead.

WOMAN. Is Lord Nasing so keen as all that?

MAN. It isn't Lord Nasing. It's our brand new editor specially imported from Chicago.

WOMAN. Will he last?

MAN. He'll last a hundred nights, say as long as the run of your piece. Then he'll get six months' screw and the boot.

WOMAN. How much is six months' screw?

MAN. Three thousand.

WOMAN. Well, I can hardly earn that myself.

MAN. Neither can I. But then you see we weren't born in Chicago.

WOMAN. I've been offered a thousand dollars a week to go there, anyhow.

MAN. Why didn't you tell me that for the interview? I've spent two entire *entr'actes* in trying to get something interesting out of you, and there you go and keep a thing like that up your sleeve. It's not fair to an old and faithful admirer. I shall stick it in. *Poulet chasseur?*

WOMAN. Oh no! Couldn't dream of it. Didn't you know I was dieting? Nothing saucy. No sugar. No bread. No tea. Thanks to that I've lost nearly a stone in six months. You know I *was* getting enormous.

MAN. Let me put *that* in, eh?

WOMAN. Just try, and see what happens to you!

MAN. Well, shall we say a lettuce salad, and a Perrier and soda? I'm dieting too.

WAITER. Lettuce salad, and a Perrier and soda? Yes, sir.

WOMAN. You aren't very gay.

MAN. Gay! You don't know all the yearnings of my soul. Don't imagine that because I'm a special of the *Record* I haven't got a soul.

WOMAN. I suppose you've been reading that book, Omar Khayyam, that everyone's talking about. Isn't that what it's called?

MAN. Has Omar Khayyam reached the theatrical world? Well, there's no doubt the earth does move, after all.

WOMAN. A little more soda, please. And just a trifle less impudence. What book ought one to be reading, then?

MAN. Socialism's the thing just now. Read Wells on Socialism. It'll be all over the theatrical world in a few years' time.

WOMAN. No fear! I can't bear Wells. He's always stirring up the dregs. I don't mind froth, but I do draw the line at dregs. What's the band playing? What have you been doing to-day? *Is* this lettuce? No, no! No bread. Didn't you hear me tell you?

MAN. I've been busy with the Priam Farll affair.

WOMAN. Priam Farll?

MAN. Yes. Painter. *You* know.

WOMAN. Oh yes. *Him!* I saw it on the posters. He's dead, it seems. Anything mysterious?

MAN. You bet! Very odd! Frightfully rich, you know! Yet he died in a wretched hovel of a place down off the Fulham Road. And his valet's disappeared. We had the first news of the death, through our arrangement with all the registrars' clerks in London. By-the-bye, don't give that away—it's our speciality. Nasing sent me off at once to write up the story.

WOMAN. Story?

MAN. The particulars. We always call it a story in Fleet Street.

WOMAN. What a good name! Well, did you find out anything interesting?

MAN. Not very much. I saw his cousin, Duncan Farll, a money-lending lawyer in Clement's Lane—he only heard of it because we telephoned to him. But the fellow would scarcely tell me anything at all.

WOMAN. Really! I do hope there's something terrible.

MAN. Why?

WOMAN. So that I can go to the inquest or the police court or whatever it is. That's why I always keep friendly with magistrates. It's so frightfully thrilling, sitting on the bench with them.

MAN. There won't be any inquest. But there's something queer in it. You see, Priam Farll was never in England. Always abroad; at those foreign hotels, wandering up and down.

WOMAN (*after a pause*). I know.

MAN. What do you know?

WOMAN. Will you promise not to chatter?

MAN. Yes.

WOMAN. I met him once at an hotel at Ostend. He—well, he wanted most tremendously to paint my portrait. But I wouldn't let him.

MAN. Why not?

WOMAN. If you knew what sort of man he was you wouldn't ask.

MAN. Oh! But look here, I say! You must let me use that in my story. Tell me all about it.

WOMAN. Not for worlds.

MAN. He—he made up to you?

WOMAN. Rather!

PRIAM FARLL (*to himself*). What a barefaced lie! Never was at Ostend in my life.

MAN. Can't I use it if I don't print your name—just say, a distinguished actress.

WOMAN. Oh yes, you can do *that*. You might say, of the musical comedy stage.

MAN. I will. I'll run something together. Trust me. Thanks awfully.

At this point a young and emaciated priest passed up the room.

WOMAN. Oh! Father Luke, is that you? Do come and sit here and be nice. This is Father Luke Widgery—Mr. Docksey, of the *Record*.

MAN. Delighted.

PRIEST. Delighted.

WOMAN. Now, Father Luke, I've just *got* to come to your sermon to-morrow. What's it about?

PRIEST. Modern vice.

WOMAN. How charming! I read the last one—it was lovely.

PRIEST. Unless you have a ticket you'll never be able to get in.

WOMAN. But I must get in. I'll come to the vestry door, if there is a vestry door at St. Bede's.

PRIEST. It's impossible. You've no idea of the crush. And I've no favourites.

WOMAN. Oh yes, you have! You have me.

PRIEST. In my church, fashionable women must take their chance with the rest.

WOMAN. How horrid you are!

PRIEST. Perhaps. I may tell you, Miss Cohenson, that I've seen two duchesses standing at the back of the aisle of St. Bede's, and glad to be there.

WOMAN. But *I* sha'n't flatter you by standing at the back of your aisle, and you needn't think it. Haven't I given you a box before now?

PRIEST. I only accepted the box as a matter of duty; it is part of my duty to go everywhere.

MAN. Come with me, Miss Cohenson. I've got two tickets for the *Record*.

WOMAN. Oh, so you do send seats to the press?

PRIEST. The press is different. Waiter, bring me half a bottle of Heidsieck.

WAITER. Half a bottle of Heidsieck? Yes, sir.

WOMAN. Heidsieck. Well, I like that. *We're* dieting.

PRIEST. *I* don't like Heidsieck. But I'm dieting too. It's my doctor's orders. Every night before retiring. It appears that my system needs it. Maria Lady Rowndell insists on giving me a hundred a year to pay for it. It is her own beautiful way of helping the good cause. Ice, please, waiter. I've just been seeing her to-night. She's staying here for the season.

Saves her a lot of trouble. She's very much cut up about the death of Priam Farll, poor thing! So artistic, you know! The late Lord Rowndell had what is supposed to be the finest lot of Farlls in England.

MAN. Did you ever meet Priam Farll, Father Luke?

PRIEST. Never. I understand he was most eccentric. I hate eccentricity. I once wrote to him to ask him if he would paint a Holy Family for St. Bede's.

MAN. And what did he reply?

PRIEST. He didn't reply. Considering that he wasn't even an R.A., I don't think that it was quite nice of him. However, Maria Lady Rowndell insists that he must be buried in Westminster Abbey. She asked me what I could do.

WOMAN. Buried in Westminster Abbey! I'd no idea he was so big as all that! Gracious!

PRIEST. I have the greatest confidence in Maria Lady Rowndell's taste, and certainly I bear no grudge. I may be able to arrange something. My uncle the Dean——

MAN. Pardon me. I always understood that since you left the Church——

PRIEST. Since I joined the Church, you mean. There is but one.

MAN. Church of England, I meant.

PRIEST. Ah!

MAN. Since you left the Church of England, there had been a breach between the Dean and yourself.

PRIEST. Merely religious. Besides my sister is the Dean's favourite niece. And I am her favourite brother. My sister takes much interest in art. She has just painted a really exquisite tea-cosy for me. Of course the Dean ultimately settles these questions of national funerals. Hence . . .

At this point the invisible orchestra began to play "God save the King."

WOMAN. Oh! What a bore!

Then nearly all the lights were extinguished.

WAITER. Please, gentlemen! Gentlemen, please!

PRIEST. You quite understand, Mr. Docksey, that I merely gave these family details in order to substantiate my statement that I may be able to arrange something. By the way, if you would care to have a typescript of my sermon to-morrow for the *Record,* you can have one by applying at the vestry.

WAITER. Please, gentlemen!

MAN. So good of you. As regards the burial in Westminster Abbey, I think that the *Record* will support the project. I say I *think.*

PRIEST. Maria Lady Rowndell will be grateful.

Five-sixths of the remaining lights went out, and the entire company followed them. In the foyer there was a prodigious crush of opera cloaks, silk hats, and cigars, all jostling together. News arrived from the Strand that the weather had turned to rain, and all the intellect of the Grand Babylon was centred upon the British climate, exactly as if the British climate had been the latest discovery of science. As the doors swung to and fro, the stridency of whistles, the throbbing of motor-cars, and the hoarse cries of inhabitants of box seats mingled strangely with the delicate babble of the interior. Then, lo! as by magic, the foyer was empty save for the denizens of the hotel who could produce evidence of identity. It had been proved to demonstration, for the sixth time that week, that in the metropolis of the greatest of Empires there is not one law for the rich and another for the poor.

Deeply affected by what he had overheard, Priam Farll rose in a lift and sought his bed. He perceived clearly that he had been among the governing classes of the realm.

CHAPTER IV.

A SCOOP.

WITHIN less than twelve hours after that conversation between members of the governing classes at the Grand Babylon Hotel, Priam Farll heard the first deep-throated echoes of the voice of England on the question of his funeral. The voice of England issued on this occasion through the mouth of the *Sunday News*, a newspaper which belonged to Lord Nasing, the proprietor of the *Daily Record*. There was a column in the *Sunday News*, partly concerning the meeting of Priam Farll and a celebrated star of the musical comedy stage at Ostend. There was also a leading article, in which it was made perfectly clear that England would stand ashamed among the nations, if she did not inter her greatest painter in Westminster Abbey. Only the article, instead of saying Westminster Abbey, said National Valhalla. It seemed to make a point of not mentioning Westminster Abbey by name, as though Westminster Abbey had been something not quite mentionable, such as a pair of trousers. The article ended with the word "basilica," and by the time you had reached this majestic substantive, you felt indeed, with the *Sunday News,* that a National Valhalla without the remains of a Priam Farll inside it, would be shocking, if not inconceivable.

Priam Farll was extremely disturbed.

On Monday morning the *Daily Record* came nobly to the support of the *Sunday News.* It had evidently spent its Sunday in collecting the opinions of a number of famous men—including three M.P.'s, a banker, a Colonial premier, a K.C., a cricketer, and the President of the Royal Academy — as to whether the National Valhalla was or was not a suitable place for the repose of the remains of Priam Farll; and the unanimous reply was in the affirmative. Other newspapers expressed the same view. But there were opponents of the scheme. Some organs coldly inquired what Priam Farll had *done* for England, and particularly for the higher life of England. He had not been a moral painter like Hogarth or Sir Noel Paton, nor a worshipper of classic legend and beauty like the unique Leighton. He had openly scorned England. He had never lived in England. He had avoided the Royal Academy, honouring every country save his own. And was he such a great painter, after all? Was he anything but a clever dauber whose work had been forced into general admiration by the efforts of a small clique of eccentric admirers? Far be it from them, the organs, to decry a dead man, but

the National Valhalla was the National Valhalla. . . .
And so on.

The penny evening papers were pro-Farll, one of
them furiously so. You gathered that if Priam Farll
was not buried in Westminster Abbey the penny evening papers would, from mere disgust, wipe their boots
on Dover cliffs and quit England eternally for some
land where art was understood. You gathered, by
nightfall, that Fleet Street must be a scene of carnage,
full of enthusiasts cutting each other's throats for the
sake of the honour of art. However, no abnormal
phenomenon was superficially observable in Fleet Street;
nor was martial law proclaimed at the Arts Club in
Dover Street. London was impassioned by the question of Farll's funeral; a few hours would decide if
England was to be shamed among the nations: and yet
the town seemed to pursue its jog-trot way exactly as
usual. The Gaiety Theatre performed its celebrated
nightly musical comedy, "House Full;" and at Queen's
Hall quite a large audience was collected to listen to
a violinist aged twelve, who played like a man, though
a little one, and whose services had been bought for
seven years by a limited company.

The next morning the controversy was settled by
one of the *Daily Record's* characteristic "scoops." In
the nature of the case, such controversies, if they are
not settled quickly, settle themselves quickly; they can-

not be prolonged. But it was the *Daily Record* that settled this one. The *Daily Record* came out with a copy of the will of Priam Farll, in which, after leaving a pound a week for life to his valet, Henry Leek, Priam Farll bequeathed the remainder of his fortune to the nation for the building and up-keep of a Gallery of Great Masters. Priam Farll's own collection of great masters, gradually made by him in that inexpensive manner which is possible only to the finest connoisseurs, was to form the nucleus of the Gallery. It comprised, said the *Record,* several Rembrandts, a Velasquez, six Vermeers, a Giorgione, a Turner, a Charles, two Cromes, a Holbein. (After Charles the *Record* put a note of interrogation, itself being uncertain of the name.) The pictures were in Paris—had been for many years. The leading idea of the Gallery was that nothing not absolutely first-class should be admitted to it. The testator attached two conditions to the bequest. One was that his own name should be inscribed nowhere in the building, and the other was that none of his own pictures should be admitted to the gallery. Was not this sublime? Was not this true British pride? Was not this magnificently unlike the ordinary benefactor of his country? The *Record* was in a position to assert that Priam Farll's estate would amount to about a hundred and forty thousand pounds, in addition to the value of the pictures. After that, was anybody going to argue that he ought not to be buried in the National Valhalla, a philanthropist so royal and so proudly meek?

The opposition gave up.

Priam Farll grew more and more disturbed in his fortress at the Grand Babylon Hotel. He perfectly remembered making the will. He had made it about seventeen years before, after some champagne in Venice, in an hour of anger against some English criticisms of his work. Yes, English criticisms! It was his vanity that had prompted him to reply in that manner. Moreover, he was quite young then. He remembered the youthful glee with which he had appointed his next-of-kin, whoever they might be, executors and trustees of the will. He remembered his cruel joy in picturing their disgust at being compelled to carry out the terms of such a will. Often, since, he had meant to destroy the will; but carelessly he had always omitted to do so. And his collection and his fortune had continued to increase regularly and mightily, and now—well, there the thing was! Duncan Farll had found the will. And Duncan Farll would be the executor and trustee of that melodramatic testament.

He could not help smiling, serious as the situation was.

During that day the thing was settled; the authorities spoke; the word went forth. Priam Farll was to be buried in Westminster Abbey on the Thursday. The dignity of England among artistic nations had been saved, partly by the heroic efforts of the *Daily Record,* and partly by the will, which proved that after all Priam Farll had had the highest interests of his country at heart.

COWARDICE.

On the night between Tuesday and Wednesday Priam Farll had not a moment of sleep. Whether it was the deep-throated voice of England that had spoken, or merely the voice of the Dean's favourite niece—so skilled in painting tea-cosies—the affair was excessively serious. For the nation was preparing to inter in the National Valhalla the remains of just Henry Leek! Priam's mind had often a sardonic turn; he was assuredly capable of strange caprices: but even he could not permit an error so gigantic to continue. The matter must be rectified, and instantly! And he alone could rectify it. The strain on his shyness would be awful, would be scarcely endurable. Nevertheless, he must act. Quite apart from other considerations, there was the consideration of that hundred and forty thousand pounds, which was his, and which he had not the slightest desire to leave to the British nation. And as for giving his beloved pictures to the race which adored

Landseer, Edwin Long, and Leighton—the idea nauseated him.

He must go and see Duncan Farll! And explain! Yes, explain that he was not dead.

Then he had a vision of Duncan Farll's hard, stupid face, and impenetrable steel head; and of himself being kicked out of the house, or delivered over to a policeman, or in some subtler way unimaginably insulted. Could he confront Duncan Farll? Was a hundred and forty thousand pounds and the dignity of the British nation worth the bearding of Duncan Farll? No! His distaste for Duncan Farll amounted to more than a hundred and forty millions of pounds and the dignity of whole planets. He felt that he could never bring himself to meet Duncan Farll. Why, Duncan might shove him into a lunatic asylum, might . . .!

Still, he must act.

Then it was that occurred to him the brilliant notion of making a clean breast of it to the Dean. He had not the pleasure of the Dean's personal acquaintance. The Dean was an abstraction; certainly much more abstract than Priam Farll. He thought he could meet the Dean. A terrific enterprise, but he must accomplish it! After all, a Dean—what was it? Nothing but a man with a funny hat! And was not he himself Priam Farll, the authentic Priam Farll, vastly greater than any Dean?

He told the valet to buy black gloves, and a silk

hat, sized seven and a quarter, and to bring up a copy of *Who's Who*. He hoped the valet would be dilatory in executing these commands. But the valet seemed to fulfil them by magic. Time flew so fast that (in a way of speaking) you could hardly see the fingers as they whirled round the clock. And almost before he knew where he was, two commissionaires were helping him into an auto-cab, and the terrific enterprise had begun. The auto-cab would easily have won the race for the Gordon Bennett Cup. It was of about two hundred h. p., and it arrived in Dean's Yard in less time than a fluent speaker would take to say Jack Robinson. The rapidity of its flight was simply incredible.

"I'll keep you," Priam Farll was going to say, as he descended, but he thought it would be more final to dismiss the machine; so he dismissed it.

He rang the bell with frantic haste, lest he should run away ere he had rung it. And then his heart went thumping, and the perspiration damped the lovely lining of his new hat; and his legs trembled, literally!

He was in hell on the Dean's door-step.

The door was opened by a man in livery of pre-latical black, who eyed him inimically.

"Er——" stammered Priam Farll, utterly flustered and craven. "Is this Mr. Parker's?"

Now Parker was not the Dean's name, and Priam

knew that it was not. Parker was merely the first name that had come into Priam's cowardly head.

"No, it isn't," said the flunkey with censorious lips. "It's the Dean's."

"Oh, I beg pardon," said Priam Farll. "I thought it was Mr. Parker's."

And he departed.

Between the ringing of the bell and the flunkey's appearance, he had clearly seen what he was capable, and what he was incapable, of doing. And the correction of England's error was among his incapacities. He could not face the Dean. He could not face anyone. He was a poltroon in all these things; a poltroon. No use arguing! He could not do it.

"I thought it was Mr. Parker's!" Good heavens! To what depths can a great artist fall.

That evening he received a cold letter from Duncan Farll, with a nave-ticket for the funeral. Duncan Farll did not venture to be sure that Mr. Henry Leek would think proper to attend his master's interment; but he enclosed a ticket. He also stated that the pound a week would be paid to him in due course. Lastly he stated that several newspaper representatives had demanded Mr. Henry Leek's address, but he had not thought fit to gratify this curiosity.

Priam was glad of that.

"Well, I'm dashed!" he reflected, handling the ticket for the nave.

There it was, large, glossy, real as life.

IN THE VALHALLA.

In the vast nave there were relatively few people—that is to say, a few hundreds, who had sufficient room to move easily to and fro under the eyes of officials. Priam Farll had been admitted through the cloisters, according to the direction printed on the ticket. In his nervous fancy, he imagined that everybody must be gazing at him suspiciously, but the fact was that he occupied the attention of no one at all. He was with the unprivileged, on the wrong side of the massive screen which separated the nave from the packed choir and transepts, and the unprivileged are never interested in themselves; it is the privileged who interest them. The organ was wafting a melody of Purcell to the furthest limits of the Abbey. Round a roped space a few ecclesiastical uniforms kept watch over the ground that would be the tomb. The sunlight of noon beat and quivered in long lances through crimson and blue windows. Then the functionaries began to form an aisle among the spectators, and emotion grew tenser. The organ was silent for a moment, and when it recommenced its song the song was the supreme ex-

pression of human grief, the dirge of Chopin, wrapping
the whole cathedral in heavy folds of sorrow. And as
that appeal expired in the pulsating air, the fresh voices
of little boys, sweeter even than grief, rose in the
distance.

It was at this point that Priam Farll descried Lady
Sophia Entwistle, a tall, veiled figure, in full mourning.
She had come among the comparatively unprivileged
to his funeral. Doubtless influence such as hers could
have obtained her a seat in the transept, but she had
preferred the secluded humility of the nave. She had
come from Paris for his funeral. She was weeping for
her affianced. She stood there, actually within ten
yards of him. She had not caught sight of him, but
she might do so at any moment, and she was slowly
approaching the spot where he trembled.

He fled, with nothing in his heart but resentment
against her. She had not proposed to him; he had
proposed to her. She had not thrown him aside; he
had thrown her aside. He was not one of her mistakes; she was one of his mistakes. Not she, but he,
had been capricious, impulsive, hasty. Yet he hated
her. He genuinely thought she had sinned against him,
and that she ought to be exterminated. He condemned
her for all manner of things as to which she had had
no choice; for instance, the irregularity of her teeth, and
the hollow under her chin, and the little tricks of de-

portment which are always developed by a spinster as
she reaches forty. He fled in terror of her. If she
should have a glimpse of him, and should recognise
him, the consequence would be absolutely disastrous—
disastrous in every way; and a period of publicity would
dawn for him such as he could not possibly contem-
plate either in cold blood or warm. He fled blindly,
insinuating himself through the crowd, until he reached
a grille in which was a gate, ajar. His strange stare
must have affrighted the guardian of the gate, for the
robed fellow stood away, and Priam passed within the
grille, where were winding steps, which he mounted.
Up the steps ran coils of fire-hose. He heard the click
of the gate as the attendant shut it, and he was thank-
ful for an escape. The steps led to the organ-loft,
perched on the top of the massive screen. The organist
was seated behind a half-drawn curtain, under shaded
electric lights, and on the ample platform whose parapet
overlooked the choir were two young men who whispered
with the organist. None of the three even glanced at
Priam. Priam sat down on a windsor chair fearfully,
like an intruder, his face towards the choir.

The whispers ceased; the organist's fingers began to
move over five rows of notes, and over scores of stops,
while his feet groped beneath, and Priam heard music,
afar off. And close behind him he heard rumblings,
steamy vibrations, and, as it were, sudden escapes of

gas; and comprehended that these were the hoarse
responses of the 32 and 64 foot pipes, laid horizontally
along the roof of the screen, to the summoning fingers
of the organist. It was all uncanny, weird, supernatural,
demoniacal if you will—it was part of the secret and
unsuspected mechanism of a vast emotional pageant
and spectacle. It unnerved Priam, especially when the
organist, a handsome youngish man with lustrous eyes,
half turned and winked at one of his companions.

The thrilling voices of the choristers grew louder,
and as they grew louder Priam Farll was conscious of
unaccustomed phenomena in his throat, which shut and
opened of itself convulsively. To divert his attention
from his throat, he partially rose from the windsor
chair, and peeped over the parapet of the screen into
the choir, whose depths were candle-lit and whose
altitudes were capriciously bathed by the intermittent
splendours of the sun. High, high up, in front of him,
at the summit of a precipice of stone, a little window,
out of the sunshine, burned sullenly in a gloom of
complicated perspectives. And far below, stretched
round the pulpit and disappearing among the forest of
statuary in the transept, was a floor consisting of the
heads of the privileged—famous, renowned, notorious,
by heredity, talent, enterprise, or hazard; he had read
many of their names in the *Daily Telegraph*. The
voices of the choristers had become piercing in their

beauty. Priam frankly stood up, and leaned over the
parapet. Every gaze was turned to a point under him
which he could not see. And then something swayed
from beneath into the field of his vision. It was a tall
cross borne by a beadle. In the wake of the cross
there came to view gorgeous ecclesiastics in pairs, and
then a robed man walking backwards and gesticulating
in the manner of some important, excited official of the
Salvation Army; and after this violent robe arrived the
scarlet choristers, singing to the beat of his gesture.
And then swung into view the coffin, covered with a
heavy purple pall, and on the pall a single white cross;
and the pall-bearers—great European names that had
hurried out of the corners of Europe as at a peremptory
mandate—with Duncan Farll to complete the tale!

Was it the coffin, or the richness of its pall, or the
solitary whiteness of its cross of flowers, or the august
authority of the bearers, that affected Priam Farll like a
blow on the heart? Who knows? But the fact was
that he could look no more; the scene was too much
for him. Had he continued to look he would have
burst uncontrollably into tears. It mattered not that
the corpse of a common rascally valet lay under that
pall; it mattered not that a grotesque error was being
enacted; it mattered not whether the actuating spring
of the immense affair was the Dean's water-colouring
niece or the solemn deliberations of the Chapter; it

mattered not that newspapers had ignobly misused the
name and honour of art for their own advancement—
the instant effect was overwhelmingly impressive. All
that had been honest and sincere in the heart of England for a thousand years leapt mystically up and made
it impossible that the effect should be other than overwhelmingly impressive. It was an effect beyond argument and reason; it was the magic flowering of
centuries in a single moment, the silent awful sigh of a
nation's secular soul. It took majesty and loveliness
from the walls around it, and rendered them again ten-
fold. It left nothing common, neither the motives nor
the littleness of men. In Priam's mind it gave dignity
to Lady Sophia Entwistle, and profound tragedy to the
death of Leek; it transformed even the gestures of the
choir-leader into grave commands.

And all that was for him! He had brushed pig-
ments onto cloth in a way of his own, nothing more,
and the nation to which he had always denied artistic
perceptions, the nation which he had always fiercely
accused of sentimentality, was thus solemnising his com-
mittal to the earth! Divine mystery of art! The large
magnificence of England smote him! He had not suspected his own greatness, nor England's.

The music ceased. He chanced to look up at the
little glooming window, perched out of reach of mankind. And the thought that the window had burned

there, patiently and unexpectantly, for hundreds of years, like an anchorite above the river and town, somehow disturbed him so that he could not continue to look at it. Ineffable sadness of a mere window! And his eye fell—fell on the coffin of Henry Leek with its white cross, and the representative of England's majesty standing beside it. And there was the end of Priam Farll's self-control. A pang like a pang of parturition itself seized him, and an issuing sob nearly ripped him in two. It was a loud sob, undisguised, unashamed, reverberating. Other sobs succeeded it. Priam Farll was in torture.

A NEW HAT.

The organist vaulted over his seat, shocked by the outrage.

"You really mustn't make that noise," whispered the organist.

Priam Farll shook him off.

The organist was apparently at a loss what to do.

"Who is it?" whispered one of the young men.

"Don't know him from Adam!" said the organist with conviction, and then to Priam Farll: "Who are you? You've no right to be here. Who gave you permission to come up here?"

And the rending sobs continued to issue from the

full-bodied ridiculous man of fifty, utterly careless of decorum.

"It's perfectly absurd!" whispered the youngster who had whispered before.

There had been a silence in the choir.

"Here! They're waiting for you!" whispered the other young man excitedly to the organist.

"By——!" whispered the alarmed organist, not stopping to say by what, but leaping like an acrobat back to his seat. His fingers and boots were at work instantly, and as he played he turned his head and whispered—

"Better fetch someone."

One of the young men crept quickly and creakingly down the stairs. Fortunately the organ and choristers were now combined to overcome the sobbing, and they succeeded. Presently a powerful arm, hidden under a black cassock, was laid on Priam's shoulder. He hysterically tried to free himself, but he could not. The cassock and the two young men thrust him downwards. They all descended together, partly walking and partly falling. And then a door was opened, and Priam discovered himself in the unroofed air of the cloisters, without his hat, and breathing in gasps. His executioners were also breathing in gasps. They glared at him in triumphant menace, as though they had done something, which indeed they had, and as though they meant to do something more but could not quite decide what.

"Where's your ticket of admission?" demanded the cassock.

Priam fumbled for it, and could not find it.

"I must have lost it," he said weakly.

"What's your name, anyhow?"

"Priam Farll," said Priam Farll, without thinking.

"Off his nut, evidently!" murmured one of the young men contemptuously. "Come on, Stan. Don't let's miss that anthem, for this cuss." And off they both went.

Then a youthful policeman appeared, putting on his helmet as he quitted the fane.

"What's all this?" asked the policeman, in the assured tone of one who had the forces of the Empire behind him.

"He's been making a disturbance in the horgan-loft," said the cassock, "and now he says his name's Priam Farll."

"Oh!" said the policeman. "Ho! And how did he get into the organ-loft?"

"Don't arsk me," answered the cassock. "He ain't got no ticket."

"Now then, out of it!" said the policeman, taking zealously hold of Priam.

"I'll thank you to leave me alone," said Priam, rebelling with all the pride of his nature against this clutch of the law.

"Oh, you will, will you?" said the policeman. "We'll see about that. We shall just see about that."

And the policeman dragged Priam along the cloister to the muffled music of "He will swallow up death in victory." They had not thus proceeded very far when they met another policeman, an older policeman.

"What's all this?" demanded the older policeman.

"Drunk and disorderly in the Abbey!" said the younger.

"Will you come quietly?" the older policeman asked Priam, with a touch of commiseration.

"I'm not drunk," said Priam fiercely; he was unversed in London, and unaware of the foolishness of reasoning with the watch-dogs of justice.

"Will you come quietly?" the older policeman repeated, this time without any touch of commiseration.

"Yes," said Priam.

And he went quietly. Experience may teach with the rapidity of lightning.

"But where's my hat?" he added after a moment, instinctively stopping.

"Now then!" said the older policeman. "Come on."

He walked between them, striding. Just as they emerged into Dean's Yard, his left hand nervously ex-

ploring one of his pockets, on a sudden encountered a
piece of card-board.

"Here's my ticket," he said. "I thought I'd lost it.
I've had nothing at all to drink, and you'd better let
me go. The whole affair's a mistake."

The procession halted, while the older policeman
gazed fascinated at the official document.

"Henry Leek," he read, deciphering the name.

"He's been a-telling everyone as he's Priam Farll,"
grumbled the younger policeman, looking over the other's
shoulder.

"I've done no such thing," said Priam promptly.

The elder carefully inspected the prisoner, and two
little boys arrived and formed a crowd, which was immediately dispersed by a frown.

"He don't look as if he'd had 'ardly as much drink
as 'ud wash a bus, does he?" murmured the elder
critically. The younger, afraid of his senior, said nothing. "Look here, Mr. Henry Leek," the elder proceeded, "do you know what I should do if I was you?
I should go and buy myself a new hat, if I was you,
and quick too!"

Priam hastened away, and heard the senior say to
the junior, "He's a toff, that's what he is, and you're a
fool. Have you forgotten as you're on point duty?"

And such is the effect of a suggestion given under
certain circumstances by a man of authority, that Priam

Farll went straight along Victoria Street and at Sowter's famous one-price hat-shop did in fact buy himself a new hat. He then hailed a taximeter from the stand opposite the Army and Navy Stores, and curtly gave the address of the Grand Babylon Hotel. And when the cab was fairly at speed, and not before, he abandoned himself to a fit of candid, unrestrained cursing. He cursed largely and variously and shamelessly both in English and in French. And he did not cease cursing. It was a reaction which I do not care to characterise; but I will not conceal that it occurred. The fit spent itself before he reached the hotel, for most of Parliament Street was blocked for the spectacular purposes of his funeral, and his driver had to seek devious ways. The cursing over, he began to smooth his plumes in detail. At the hotel, out of sheer nervousness, he gave the cabman half-a-crown, which was preposterous.

Another cab drove up nearly at the exact instant of his arrival. And, as a capping to the day, Mrs. Alice Challice stepped out of it.

CHAPTER V.

ALICE ON HOTELS.

SHE was wearing the same red roses.

"Oh!" she said, very quickly, pouring out the words generously from the inexhaustible mine of her good heart. "I'm so sorry I missed you Saturday night. I can't tell you how sorry I am. Of course it was all my fault. I oughtn't to have got into the lift without you. I ought to have waited. When I was in the lift I wanted to get out, but the lift-man was too quick for me. And then on the platforms—well, there was such a crowd it was useless! I knew it was useless. And you not having my address either! I wondered whatever you would think of me."

"My dear lady!" he protested. "I can assure you I blamed only myself. My hat blew off, and——"

"Did it now!" she took him up breathlessly. "Well, all I want you to understand really is that I'm not one of those silly sort of women that go losing themselves. No. Such a thing's never happened to me before, and I shall take good care——"

She glanced round. He had paid both the cabmen,

who were departing, and he and Mrs. Alice Challice
stood under the immense glass portico of the Grand
Babylon, exposed to the raking stare of two commissionaires.

"So you *are* staying here!" she said, as if laying
hold of a fact which she had hitherto hesitated to
touch.

"Yes," he said. "Won't you come in?"

He took her into the rich gloom of the Grand
Babylon dashingly, fighting against the demon of shyness
and beating it off with great loss. They sat down in a
corner of the principal foyer, where a few electric lights
drew attention to empty fauteuils and the blossoms on
the Aubusson carpet. The world was at lunch.

"And a fine time I had getting your address!" said
she. "Of course I wrote at once to Selwood Terrace,
as soon as I got home, but I had the wrong number,
somehow, and I kept waiting and waiting for an answer,
and the only answer I received was the returned letter.
I knew I'd got the street right, and I said, 'I'll find that
house if I have to ring every bell in Selwood Terrace,
yes, and knock every knocker!' Well, I did find it,
and then they wouldn't *give* me your address. They
said 'letters would be forwarded,' if you please. But I
wasn't going to have any more letter business, no, thank
you! So I said I wouldn't go without the address. It
was Mr. Duncan Farll's clerk that I saw. He's living

there for the time being. A very nice young man. We got quite friendly. It seems Mr. Duncan Farll *was* in a state when he found the will. The young man did say that he broke a typewriter all to pieces. But the funeral being in Westminster Abbey consoled him. It wouldn't have consoled me—no, not it! However, he's very rich himself, so that doesn't matter. The young man said if I'd call again he'd ask his master if he might give me your address. A rare fuss over an address, thought I to myself. But there! Lawyers! So I called again, and he gave it me. I could have come yesterday. I very nearly wrote last night. But I thought on the whole I'd better wait till the funeral was over. I thought it would be nicer It's over now, I suppose?"

"Yes," said Priam Farll.

She smiled at him with grave sympathy, comfortably and sensibly. "And right down relieved you must be!" she murmured. "It must have been very trying for you."

"In a way," he answered hesitatingly, "it was."

Taking off her gloves, she glanced round about her, as a thief must glance before opening the door, and then, leaning suddenly towards him, she put her hands to his neck and touched his collar. "No, no!" she said. "Let me do it. I can do it. There's no one looking. It's unbuttoned; the necktie was holding it in place, but it's got quite loose now. There! I can do it. I see you've got two funny moles on your neck, close together. How lucky! That's it!" A final pat!

Now, no woman had ever patted Priam Farll's necktie before, much less buttoned his collar, and still much less referred to the two little moles, one hirsute, the other hairless, which the collar hid—when it was properly buttoned! The experience was startling for him in the extreme. It might have made him very angry, had the hands of Mrs. Challice not been—well, nurse's hands, soft hands, persuasive hands, hands that could practise impossible audacities with impunity. Imagine a woman, uninvited and unpermitted, arranging his collar and necktie for him in the largest public room of the Grand Babylon, and then talking about his little moles! It would have been unimaginable! Yet it happened. And moreover, he had not disliked it. She sat back in her chair as though she had done nothing in the least degree unusual.

"I can see you must have been very upset," she said gently, "though he *has* only left you a pound a week. Still, that's better than a bat in the eye with a burnt stick."

A bat in the eye with a burnt stick reminded him vaguely of encounters with the police; otherwise it conveyed no meaning to his mind.

"I hope you haven't got to go on duty at once,"

she said after a pause. "Because you really do look as if you needed a rest, and a cup of tea or something of that. I'm quite ashamed to have come bothering you so soon."

"Duty?" he questioned. "What duty?"

"Why," she exclaimed, "haven't you got a new place?"

"New place!" he repeated after. "What do you mean?"

"Why, as valet."

There was certainly danger in his tendency to forget that he was a valet. He collected himself.

"No," he said, "I haven't got a new place."

"Then why are you staying here?" she cried. "I thought you were simply here with a new master. Why are you staying here alone?".

"Oh," he replied, abashed, "it seemed a convenient place. It was just by chance that I came here."

"Convenient place indeed!" she said stoutly. "I never heard of such a thing!"

He perceived that he had shocked her, pained her. He saw that some ingenious defence of himself was required; but he could find none. So he said, in his confusion—

"Suppose we go and have something to eat? I do want a bit of lunch, as you say, now I come to think of it. Will you?"

"What? Here?" she demanded apprehensively.

"Yes," he said. "Why not?"

"Well——"

"Come along!" he said, with fine casualness, and conducted her to the eight swinging glass doors that led to the *salle à manger* of the Grand Babylon. At each pair of doors was a living statue of dignity in cloth of gold. She passed these statues without a sign of fear, but when she saw the room itself, steeped in a supra-genteel calm, full of gowns and hats and everything that you read about in the *Lady's Pictorial,* and the pennoned mast of a barge crossing the windows at the other end, she stopped suddenly. And one of the lord mayors of the Grand Babylon, wearing a mayoral chain, who had started out to meet them, stopped also.

"No!" she said. "I don't feel as if I could eat here. I really couldn't."

"But why?"

"Well," she said, "I couldn't fancy it somehow. Can't we go somewhere else?"

"Certainly we can," he agreed with an eagerness that was more than polite.

She thanked him with another of her comfortable, sensible smiles—a smile that took all embarrassment out of the dilemma, as balm will take irritation from a wound. And gently she removed her hat and gown, and her gestures and speech, and her comfortableness,

from those august precincts. And they descended to
the grill-room, which was relatively noisy, and where
her roses were less conspicuous than the helmet of
Navarre, and her frock found its sisters and cousins
from far lands.

"I'm not much for these restaurants," she said, over
grilled kidneys.

"No?" he responded tentatively. "I'm sorry. I
thought the other night——"

"Oh yes," she broke in, "I was very glad to go, the
other night, to that place, very glad. But, you see, I'd
never been in a restaurant before."

"Really?"

"No," she said, "and I felt as if I should like to
try one. And the young lady at the post office had
told me that *that* one was a splendid one. So it is.
It's beautiful. But of course they ought to be ashamed
to offer you such food. Now do you remember that
sole? Sole! It was no more sole than this glove's
sole. And if it had been cooked a minute, it had
been cooked an hour, and waiting. And then look at
the prices. Oh yes, I couldn't help seeing the bill."

"I thought it was awfully cheap," said he.

"Well, *I* didn't!" said she. "When you think that
a good housekeeper can keep everything going on ten
shillings a head a *week*. . . . Why, it's simply scandalous! And I suppose this place is even dearer?"

He avoided the question. "This is a better place altogether," he said. "In fact, I don't know many places in Europe where one can eat better than one does here."

"Don't you?" she said indulgently, as if saying, "Well, I know one, at any rate."

"They say," he continued, "that there is no butter used in this place that costs less than three shillings a pound."

"*No* butter costs them three shillings a pound," said she.

"Not in London," said he. "They have it from Paris."

"And do you believe that?" she asked.

"Yes," he said.

"Well, I don't. Anyone that pays more than one-and-nine a pound for butter, *at the most,* is a fool, if you'll excuse me saying the word. Not but what this is good butter. I couldn't get as good in Putney for less than eighteen pence."

She made him feel like a child who has a great deal to pick up from a kindly but firm sister.

"No, thank you," she said, a little dryly, to the waiter who proffered a further supply of chip potatoes.

"Now don't say they're cold," Priam laughed.

And she laughed also. "Shall I tell you one thing that puts me against these restaurants?" she went on.

"It's the feeling you have that you don't know where the food's *been*.   When you've got your kitchen close to your dining-room, and you can keep an eye on the stuff from the moment the cart brings it, well, then, you do know a bit where you are.   And you can have your dishes served hot.   It stands to reason," she said. "Where is the kitchen here?"

"Somewhere down below," he replied apologetically.

"A cellar kitchen!" she exclaimed.   "Why, in Putney they simply can't let houses with cellar kitchens. No!   No restaurants and hotels for me—not for *choice* —that is, regularly."

"Still," he said, with a judicial air, "hotels are very convenient."

"Are they?" she said, meaning, "Prove it."

"For instance, here, there's a telephone in every room."

"You don't mean in the bedrooms?"

"Yes, in every bedroom."

"Well," she said, "you wouldn't catch me having a telephone in my bedroom.   I should never sleep if I knew there was a telephone in the room!   Fancy being forced to telephone every time you want—well!   And how is one to know who there is at the other end of the telephone?   No, I don't like that.   All that's all very well for gentlemen that haven't been used to what I call *com*fort, in a way of speaking.   But——"

He saw that if he persisted, nothing soon would be left of that noble pile, the Grand Babylon Hotel, save a heap of ruins. And, further, she genuinely did cause him to feel that throughout his career he had always missed the very best things of life, through being an uncherished, ingenuous, easily satisfied man. A new sensation for him! For if any male in Europe believed in his own capacity to make others make him comfortable, Priam Farll was that male.

"I've never been in Putney," he ventured, on a new track.

DIFFICULTY OF TRUTH-TELLING.

As she informed him, with an ungrudging particularity, about Putney, and her life at Putney, there gradually arose in his brain a vision of a kind of existence such as he had never encountered. Putney had clearly the advantages of a residential town in a magnificent situation. It lay on the slope of a hill whose foot was washed by a glorious stream entitled the Thames, its breast covered with picturesque barges and ornamental rowing boats; an arched bridge spanned this stream, and you went over the bridge in milk-white omnibuses to London. Putney had a street of handsome shops, a purely business street; no one slept there

now because of the noise of motors; at eventide the
street glittered in its own splendours. There were
theatre, music-hall, assembly-rooms, concert hall, market,
brewery, library, and an afternoon tea shop exactly like
Regent Street (not that Mrs. Challice cared for their
alleged China tea); also churches and chapels; and
Barnes Common if you walked one way, and Wimbledon
Common if you walked another. Mrs. Challice lived in
Werter Road, Werter Road starting conveniently at the
corner of the High Street where the fish-shop was—an
establishment where authentic sole was always obtainable, though it was advisable not to buy it on Monday
mornings, of course. Putney was a place where you
lived unvexed, untroubled. You had your little house,
and your furniture, and your ability to look after yourself at all ends, and your knowledge of the prices of
everything, and your deep knowledge of human nature,
and your experienced forgivingness towards human
frailties. You did not keep a servant, because servants
were so complicated, and because they could do nothing
whatever as well as you could do it yourself. You had
a charwoman when you felt idle or when you chose to
put the house into the back-yard for an airing. With
the charwoman, a pair of gloves for coarser work, and
gas stoves, you "made naught" of domestic labour.
You were never worried by ambitions, or by envy, or by
the desire to know precisely what the wealthy did and

to do likewise. You read when you were not more amusingly occupied, preferring illustrated papers and magazines. You did not traffic with art to any appreciable extent, and you never dreamed of letting it keep you awake at night. You were rich, for the reason that you spent less than you received. You never speculated about the ultimate causes of things, or puzzled yourself concerning the possible developments of society in the next hundred years. When you saw a poor old creature in the street you bought a box of matches off the poor old creature. The social phenomenon which chiefly roused you to just anger was the spectacle of wealthy people making money and so taking the bread out of the mouths of people who needed it. The only apparent blots on existence at Putney were the noise and danger of the High Street, the dearth of reliable laundries, the manners of a middle-aged lady engaged at the post office (Mrs. Challice liked the other ladies in the post office), and the absence of a suitable man in the house.

Existence at Putney seemed to Priam Farll to approach the Utopian. It seemed to breathe of romance —the romance of commonsense and kindliness and simplicity. It made his own existence to that day appear a futile and unhappy striving after the impossible. Art? What was it? What did it lead to? He was sick of art, and sick of all the forms of activity to which

he had hitherto been accustomed and which he had
mistaken for life itself.

One little home, fixed and stable, rendered foolish
the whole concourse of European hotels.

"I suppose you won't be staying here long,"
demanded Mrs. Challice.

"Oh no!" he said.   "I shall decide something."

"Shall you take another place?" she inquired.

"Another place?"

"Yes."   Her smile was excessively persuasive and
inviting.

"I don't know," he said diffidently.

"You must have put a good bit by," she said, still
with the same smile.   "Or perhaps you haven't.
Saving's a matter of chance.   That's what I always do
say.   It just depends how you begin.   It's a habit.   I'd
never really blame anybody for not saving.   And
men——!"   She seemed to wish to indicate that men
were specially to be excused if they did not save.

She had a large mind: that was sure.   She understood—things, and human nature in particular.   She
was not one of those creatures that a man meets with
sometimes—creatures who are for ever on the watch to
pounce, and who are incapable of making allowances
for any male frailty—smooth, smiling creatures, with
thin lips, hair a little scanty at the front, and a quietly
omniscient "don't-tell-*me*" tone.   Mrs. Alice Challice had

a mouth as wide as her ideas, and a full underlip. She was a woman who, as it were, ran out to meet you when you started to cross the dangerous roadway which separates the two sexes. She comprehended because she wanted to comprehend. And when she could not comprehend she would deceive herself that she did: which amounts to the equivalent.

She was a living proof that in her sex social distinctions do not effectively count. Nothing counted, where she was concerned, except a distinction far more profound than any social distinction—the historic distinction between Adam and Eve. She was balm to Priam Farll. She might have been equally balm to King David, Uriah the Hittite, Socrates, Rousseau, Lord Byron, Heine, or Charlie Peace. She would have understood them all. They would all have been ready to cushion themselves on her comfortableness. Was she a lady? Pish! She was a woman.

Her temperament drew Priam Farll like an electrified magnet. To wander about freely in that roomy sympathy of hers seemed to him to be the supreme reward of experience. It seemed like the good inn after the bleak highroad, the oasis after the sandstorm, shade after glare, the dressing after the wound, sleep after insomnia, surcease from unspeakable torture. He wanted, in a word, to tell her everything, because she would not demand any difficult explanations. She had given him an opening, in her mention of savings. In reply to her suggestion, "You must have put a good bit by," he could casually answer:

"Yes, a hundred and forty thousand pounds."

And that would lead by natural stages to a complete revealing of the fix in which he was. In five minutes he would have confided to her the principal details, and she would have understood, and then he could describe his agonising and humiliating half-hour in the Abbey, and she would pour her magic oil on that dreadful abrasion of his sensitiveness. And he would be healed of his hurts, and they would settle between them what he ought to do.

He regarded her as his refuge, as fate's generous compensation to him for the loss of Henry Leek (whose remains now rested in the National Valhalla).

Only, it would be necessary to begin the explanation, so that one thing might by natural stages lead to another. On reflection, it appeared rather abrupt to say:

"Yes, a hundred and forty thousand pounds."

The sum was too absurdly high (though correct). The mischief was that, unless the sum did strike her as absurdly high, it could not possibly lead by a natural stage to the remainder of the explanation.

He must contrive another path. For instance—

"There's been a mistake about the so-called death of Priam Farll."

"A mistake!" she would exclaim, all ears and eyes. Then he would say—

"Yes. Priam Farll isn't really dead. It's his valet that's dead."

Whereupon she would burst out—

"But *you* were his valet!"

Whereupon he would simply shake his head, and she would steam forwards—

"Then who are you?"

Whereupon he would say, as calmly as he could—

"I'm Priam Farll. I'll tell you precisely how it all happened."

Thus the talk might happen. Thus it would happen, immediately he began. But, as at the Dean's door in Dean's Yard, so now, he could not begin. He could not utter the necessary words aloud. Spoken aloud, they would sound ridiculous, incredible, insane—and not even Mrs. Challice could reasonably be expected to grasp their import, much less believe them.

"*There's been a mistake about the so-called death of Priam Farll.*"

"*Yes, a hundred and forty thousand pounds.*"

No, he could enunciate neither the one sentence nor the other. There are some truths so bizarre that they make you feel self-conscious and guilty before you have

8*

begun to state them; you state them apologetically; you
blush; you stammer; you have all the air of one who
does not expect belief; you look a fool; you feel a fool;
and you bring disaster on yourself.

He perceived with the most painful clearness that
he could never, never impart to her the terrific secret,
the awful truth. Great as she was, the truth was
greater, and she would never be able to swallow it.

"What time is it?" she asked suddenly.

"Oh, you mustn't think about time," he said, with
hasty concern.

RESULTS OF RAIN.

When the lunch was completely finished and the
grill-room had so far emptied that it was inhabited by
no one except themselves and several waiters who were
trying to force them to depart by means of thought
transference and uneasy hovering round their table,
Priam Farll began to worry his brains in order to find
some sane way of spending the afternoon in her
society. He wanted to keep her, but he did not know
how to keep her. He was quite at a loss. Strange
that a man great enough and brilliant enough to get
buried in Westminster Abbey had not sufficient of the
small change of cleverness to retain the company of a

Mrs. Alice Challice! Yet so it was. Happily he was buoyed up by the thought that she understood.

"I must be moving off home," she said, putting her gloves on slowly; and sighed.

"Let me see," he stammered. "I think you said Werter Road, Putney?"

"Yes. No. 29."

"Perhaps you'll let me call on you," he ventured.

"Oh, do!" she encouraged him.

Nothing could have been more correct, and nothing more banal, than this part of their conversation. He certainly would call. He would travel down to the idyllic Putney to-morrow. He could not lose such a friend, such a balm, such a soft cushion, such a comprehending intelligence. He would bit by bit become intimate with her, and perhaps ultimately he might arrive at the stage of being able to tell her who he was with some chance of being believed. Anyhow, when he did call—and he insisted to himself that it should be extremely soon—he would try another plan with her; he would carefully decide beforehand just what to say and how to say it. This decision reconciled him somewhat to a temporary parting from her.

So he paid the bill, under her sagacious, protesting eyes, and he managed to conceal from those eyes the precise amount of the tip; and then, at the cloak-room, he furtively gave sixpence to a fat and wealthy man who had been watching over his hat and stick. (Highly curious, how those commonsense orbs of hers made all such operations seem excessively silly!) And at last they wandered, in silence, through the corridors and antechambers that led to the courtyard entrance. And through the glass portals Priam Farll had a momentary glimpse of the reflection of light on a cabman's wet macintosh. It was raining. It was raining very heavily indeed. All was dry under the glass-roofed colonnades of the courtyard, but the rain rattled like kettledrums on that glass, and the centre of the courtyard was a pond in which a few hansoms were splashing about. Everything—the horses' coats, the cabmen's hats and capes, and the cabmen's red faces, shone and streamed in the torrential summer rain. It is said that geography makes history. In England, and especially in London, weather makes a good deal of history. Impossible to brave that rain, except under the severest pressure of necessity! They were in shelter, and in shelter they must remain.

He was glad, absurdly and splendidly glad.

"It can't last long," she said, looking up at the black sky, which showed an edge towards the east.

"Suppose we go in again and have some tea?" he said.

Now they had barely concluded coffee. But she did not seem to mind.

"Well," she said, "it's always tea-time for *me.*"

He saw a clock. "It's nearly four," he said.

Thus justified of the clock, in they went, and sat down in the same seats which they had occupied at the commencement of the adventure in the main lounge. Priam discovered a bell-push, and commanded China tea and muffins. He felt that he now, as it were, had an opportunity of making a fresh start in life. He grew almost gay. He could be gay without sinning against decorum, for Mrs. Challice's singular tact had avoided all reference to deaths and funerals.

And in the pause, while he was preparing to be gay, attractive, and in fact his true self, she, calmly stirring China tea, shot a bolt which made him see stars.

"It seems to me," she observed, "that we might go farther and fare worse—both of us."

He genuinely did not catch the significance of it in the first instant, and she saw that he did not.

"Oh," she proceeded, benevolently and reassuringly, "I mean it. I'm not gallivanting about. I mean that if you want my opinion I fancy we could make a match of it."

It was at this point that he saw stars. He also saw a faint and delicious blush on her face, whose complexion was extraordinarily fresh and tender.

She sipped China tea, holding each finger wide apart from the others.

He had forgotten the origin of their acquaintance, forgotten that each of them was supposed to have a definite aim in view, forgotten that it was with a purpose that they had exchanged photographs. It had not occurred to him that marriage hung over him like a sword. He perceived the sword now, heavy and sharp, and suspended by a thread of appalling fragility. He dodged. He did not want to lose her, never to see her again; but he dodged.

"I couldn't think——" he began, and stopped.

"Of course it's a very awkward situation for a man," she went on, toying with a muffin. "I can quite understand how you feel. And with most folks you'd be right. There's very few women that can judge character, and if you started to try and settle something at once they'd just set you down as a wrong 'un. But I'm not like that. I don't expect any fiddle-faddle. What I like is plain sense and plain dealing. We both want to get married, so it would be silly to pretend we didn't, wouldn't it? And it would be ridiculous of me to look for courting and a proposal, and all that sort of thing, just as if I'd never seen a man in his shirt-sleeves. The only question is: shall we suit each other? I've told you what I think. What do you think?"

She smiled, honestly, kindly, but piercingly.

What could he say? What would you have said, you being a man? It is easy, sitting there in your chair, with no Mrs. Alice Challice in front of you, to invent diplomatic replies; but conceive yourself in Priam's place! Besides, he did think she would suit him. And most positively he could not bear the prospect of seeing her pass out of his life. He had been through that experience once, when his hat blew off in the Tube; and he did not wish to repeat it.

"Of course you've got no *home!*" she said reflectively, with such compassion. "Suppose you come down and just have a little peep at mine?"

So that evening, a suitably paired couple chanced into the fishmonger's at the corner of Werter Road, and bought a bit of sole. At the newspaper shop next door but one, placards said: "Impressive Scenes at Westminster Abbey," "Farll funeral, stately pageant," "Great painter laid to rest," etc.

CHAPTER VI.

A PUTNEY MORNING.

EXCEPT that there was marrying and giving in marriage, it was just as though he had died and gone to heaven. Heaven is the absence of worry and of ambition. Heaven is where you want nothing you haven't got. Heaven is finality. And this was finality. On the September morning, after the honeymoon and the settling down, he arose leisurely, long after his wife, and, putting on the puce dressing-gown (which Alice much admired), he opened the window wider and surveyed that part of the universe which was comprised in Werter Road and the sky above. A sturdy old woman was coming down the street with a great basket of assorted flowers; he took an immense pleasure in the sight of the old woman; the sight of the old woman thrilled him. Why? Well, there was no reason, except that she was vigorously alive, a part of the magnificent earth. All life gave him joy; all life was beautiful to him. He had his warm bath; the bathroom was not of the latest convenience, but Alice could have made a four-wheeler convenient. As he passed to and fro on the first-floor he heard the calm, efficient activities below stairs. She was busy in the mornings; her eyes would seem to say to him, "Now, between my uprising and lunch-time please don't depend on me for intellectual or moral support. I am on the spot, but I am also at the wheel and must not be disturbed."

Then he descended, fresh as a boy, although the promontory which prevented a direct vision of his toes showed accretions. The front-room was a shrine for his breakfast. She served it herself, in her white apron, promptly on his arrival! Eggs! Toast! Coffee! It was nothing, that breakfast; and yet it was everything. No breakfast could have been better. He had probably eaten about fifteen thousand hotel breakfasts before Alice taught him what a real breakfast was. After serving it she lingered for a moment, and then handed him the *Daily Telegraph,* which had been lying on a chair.

"Here's your *Telegraph,*" she said cheerfully, tacitly disowning any property or interest in the *Telegraph.* For her, newspapers were men's toys. She never opened a paper, never wanted to know what was going on in the world. She was always intent upon her own affairs. Politics—and all that business of the mere machinery of living: she perfectly ignored it! She lived. She did nothing but live. She lived every hour. Priam felt truly that he had at last got down to the bed-rock of life.

There were twenty pages of the *Telegraph,* far more matter than a man could read in a day even if he read and read and neither ate nor slept. And all of it so soothing in its rich variety! It gently lulled you; it was the ideal companion for a poached egg; upstanding against the coffee-pot, it stood for the solidity of Eng-land in the seas. Priam folded it large; he read all the articles down to the fold; then turned the thing over, and finished all of them. After communing with the *Telegraph,* he communed with his own secret nature, and wandered about, rolling a cigarette. Ah! The first cigarette! His wanderings led him to the kitchen, or at least as far as the threshold thereof. His wife was at work there. Upon every handle or article that might soil she put soft brown paper, and in addition she often wore house-gloves; so that her hands remained immacu-late; thus during the earlier hours of the day the house, especially in the region of fireplaces, had the air of being in curl-papers.

"I'm going out now, Alice," he said, after he had drawn on his finely polished boots.

"Very well, love," she replied, preoccupied with her work. "Lunch as usual." She never demanded uxo-riousness from him. She had got him. She was sure of him. That satisfied her. Sometimes, like a simple woman who has come into a set of pearls, she would, as it were, take him out of his drawer and look at him, and put him back.

At the gate he hesitated whether to turn to the left, towards High Street, or to the right, towards Oxford Road. He chose the right, but he would have enjoyed himself equally had he chosen the left. The streets through which he passed were populated by domestic servants and tradesmen's boys. He saw white-capped girls cleaning door-knobs or windows, or running along the streets, like escaped nuns, or staring in soft meditation from bedroom windows. And the tradesmen's boys were continually leaping in and out of carts, or off and on tricycles, busily distributing food and drink, as though Putney had been a beleaguered city. It was extremely interesting and mysterious—and what made it the most mysterious was that the oligarchy of superior persons for whom these boys and girls so assiduously worked, remained invisible. He passed a newspaper shop and found his customary delight in the placards. This morning the *Daily Illustrated* announced nothing but: "Portrait of a boy aged 12 who weighs 20 stone." And the *Record* whispered in scarlet: "What the German said to the King. Special." The *Journal* cried: "Surrey's glorious finish." And the *Courier* shouted: "The Unwritten Law in the United States. Another Scandal."

Not for gold would he have gone behind these placards to the organs themselves; he preferred to

gather from the placards alone what wonders of yesterday the excellent staid *Telegraph* had unaccountably
missed. But in the *Financial Times* he saw: "Cohoon's
Annual Meeting. Stormy Scenes." And he bought the
Financial Times and put it into his pocket for his wife,
because she had an interest in Cohoon's Brewery, and
he conceived the possibility of her caring to glance at
the report.

THE SIMPLE JOY OF LIFE.

After crossing the South-Western Railway he got
into the Upper Richmond Road, a thoroughfare which
always diverted and amused him. It was such a street
of contrasts. Anyone could see that, not many years
before, it had been a sacred street, trod only by feet
genteel, and made up of houses each christened with
its own name and each standing in its own garden.
And now energetic persons had put churches into it,
vast red things with gigantic bells, and large drapery
shops, with blouses at six-and-eleven, and court photo-
graphers, and banks, and cigar-stores, and auctioneers'
offices. And all kinds of omnibuses ran along it. And
yet somehow it remained meditative and superior. In
every available space gigantic posters were exhibited.
They all had to do with food or pleasure. There were
York hams eight feet high, that a regiment could not

have eaten in a month; shaggy and ferocious oxen peeping out of monstrous tea-cups in their anxiety to be consumed; spouting bottles of ale whose froth alone would have floated the mail steamers pictured on an adjoining sheet; and forty different decoctions for imparting strength. Then after a few score yards of invitation to debauch there came, with characteristic admirable English commonsense, a cure for indigestion, so large that it would have given ease to a mastodon who had by inadvertence swallowed an elephant. And then there were the calls to pleasure. Astonishing, the quantity of palaces that offered you exactly the same entertainment twice over on the same night! Astonishing, the reliance on number in this matter of amusement! Authenticated statements that a certain performer had done a certain thing in a certain way a thousand and one times without interruption were stuck all over the Upper Richmond Road, apparently in the sure hope that you would rush to see the thousand and second performance. These performances were invariably styled original and novel. All the remainder of free wall space was occupied by philanthropists who were ready to give away cigarettes at the nominal price of a penny a packet.

Priam Farll never tired of the phantasmagoria of Upper Richmond Road. The interminable, intermittent vision of food dead and alive, and of performers per-

forming the same performance from everlasting to everlasting, and of millions and millions of cigarettes as-
cending from the mouths of handsome young men in
incense to heaven—this rare vision, of which in all his
wanderings he had never seen the like, had the singular
effect of lulling his soul into a profound content. Not
once did he arrive at the end of the vision. No! when
he reached Barnes Station he could see the vision still
stretching on and on; but, filled to the brim, he would
get into an omnibus and return. The omnibus awoke
him to other issues: the omnibus was an antidote. In
the omnibus cleanliness was nigh to godliness. On one
pane a soap was extolled, and on another the exordium,
"For this is a true saying and worthy of all accepta-
tion," was followed by the statement of a religious
dogma; while on another pane was an urgent appeal
not to do in the omnibus what you would not do in a
drawing-room. Yes, Priam Farll had seen the world,
but he had never seen a city so incredibly strange, so
packed with curious and rare psychological interest as
London. And he regretted that he had not discovered
London earlier in his lifelong search after romance.

At the corner of the High Street he left the omnibus and stopped a moment to chat with his tobacconist.
His tobacconist was a stout man in a white apron, who
stood for ever behind a counter and sold tobacco to the
most respected residents of Putney. All his ideas were

connected either with tobacco or with Putney. A murder
in the Strand to that tobacconist was less than the
breakdown of a motor bus opposite Putney Station; and
a change of government less than a change of pro-
gramme at the Putney Empire. A rather pessimistic
tobacconist, not inclined to believe in a First Cause,
until one day a drunken man smashed Salmon and
Gluckstein's window down the High Street, whereupon
his opinion of Providence went up for several days!
Priam enjoyed talking to him, though the tobacconist
was utterly impervious to ideas and never gave out
ideas. This morning the tobacconist was at his door.
At the other corner was the sturdy old woman whom
Priam had observed from his window. She sold flowers.

"Fine old woman, that!" said Priam heartily, after
he and the tobacconist had agreed upon the fact that
it was a glorious morning.

"She used to be at the opposite corner by the station until last May but one, when the police shifted
her," said the tobacconist.

"Why did the police shift her?" asked Priam.

"I don't know as I can tell you," said the tobacconist. "But I remember her this twelve year."

"I only noticed her this morning," said Priam. "I
saw her from my bedroom window, coming down the
Werter Road. I said to myself, 'She's the finest old
woman I ever saw in my life!'"

"Did you now!" murmured the tobacconist. "She's rare and dirty."

"I like her to be dirty," said Priam stoutly. "She ought to be dirty. She wouldn't be the same if she were clean."

"I don't hold with dirt," said the tobacconist calmly. "She'd be better if she had a bath of a Saturday night like other folks."

"Well," said Priam, "I want an ounce of the usual."

"Thank *you,* sir," said the tobacconist, putting down three-halfpence change out of sixpence as Priam thanked him for the packet.

Nothing whatever in such a dialogue! Yet Priam left the shop with a distinct feeling that life was good. And he plunged into High Street, lost himself in crowds of perambulators and nice womanly women who were bustling honestly about in search of food or raiment. Many of them carried little red books full of long lists of things which they and their admirers and the off-spring of mutual affection had eaten or would shortly eat. In the High Street all was luxury: not a necessary in the street. Even the bakers' shops were a mass of sultana and Berlin pancakes. Illuminated calendars, gramophones, corsets, picture postcards, Manilla cigars, bridge-scorers, chocolate, exotic fruit, and commodious mansions—these seemed to be the principal objects offered for sale in High Street. Priam bought a sixpenny edition of Herbert Spencer's *Essays* for fourpence-halfpenny, and passed on to Putney Bridge, whose noble arches divided a first storey of vans and omnibuses from a ground-floor of barges and racing eights. And he gazed at the broad river and its hanging gardens, and dreamed; and was wakened by the roar of an electric train shooting across the stream on a red cause-way a few yards below him. And, miles off, he could descry the twin towers of the Crystal Palace, more mar-vellous than mosques!

"Astounding!" he murmured joyously. He had not a care in the world; and Putney was all that Alice had painted it. In due time, when bells had pealed to right and to left of him, he went home to her.

COLLAPSE OF THE PUTNEY SYSTEM.

Now, just at the end of lunch, over the last stage of which they usually sat a long time, Alice got up quickly, in the midst of her Stilton, and, going to the mantelpiece, took a letter therefrom.

"I wish you'd look at that, Henry," she said, hand-ing him the letter. "It came this morning, but of course I can't be bothered with that sort of thing in the morn-ing. So I put it aside."

He accepted the letter, and unfolded it with the professional all-knowing air which even the biggest male

fool will quite successfully put on in the presence of a
woman if consulted about business.   When he had unfolded the thing—it was typed on stiff, expensive, quarto
paper—he read it.   In the lives of beings like Priam
Farll and Alice a letter such as that letter is a terrible
event, unique, earth-arresting; simple recipients are apt,
on receiving it, to imagine that the Christian era has
come to an end.   But tens of thousands of similar
letters are sent out from the City every day, and the
City thinks nothing of them.

The letter was about Cohoon's Brewery Company,
Limited, and it was signed by a firm of solicitors.   It
referred to the verbatim report, which it said would be
found in the financial papers, of the annual meeting of
the company held at the Cannon Street Hotel on the
previous day, and to the exceedingly unsatisfactory
nature of the Chairman's statement.   It regretted the
absence of Mrs. Alice Challice (her change of condition
had not yet reached the heart of Cohoon's) from the
meeting, and asked her whether she would be prepared
to support the action of a committee which had been
formed to eject the existing board and which had
already a following of 385,000 votes.   It finished by
asserting that unless the committee was immediately
lifted to absolute power the company would be quite
ruined.

Priam re-read the letter aloud.

"What does it all mean?" asked Alice quietly.

"Well," said he, "that's what it means."

"Does it mean——?" she began.

"By Jove!" he exclaimed, "I forgot. I saw something on a placard this morning about Cohoon's, and I thought it might interest you, so I bought it." So saying, he drew from his pocket the *Financial Times,* which he had entirely forgotten. There it was: a column and a quarter of the Chairman's speech, and nearly two columns of stormy scenes. The Chairman was the Marquis of Drumgaldy, but his rank had apparently not shielded him from the violence of expletives such as "Liar!" "Humbug!" and even "Rogue!" The Marquis had merely stated, with every formula of apology, that, owing to the extraordinary depreciation in licensed property, the directors had not felt justified in declaring any dividend at all on the Ordinary Shares of the company. He had made this quite simple assertion, and instantly a body of shareholders, less reasonable and more avaricious even than shareholders usually are, had begun to turn the historic hall of the Cannon Street Hotel into a bear garden. One might have imagined that the sole aim of brewery companies was to make money, and that the patriotism of old-world brewers, that patriotism which impelled them to supply an honest English beer to the honest English working-

man at a purely nominal price, was scorned and forgotten. One was, indeed, forced to imagine this. In
vain the Marquis pointed out that the shareholders had
received a fifteen per cent. dividend for years and years
past, and that really, for once in a way, they ought to
be prepared to sacrifice a temporary advantage for the
sake of future prosperity. The thought of those regular
high dividends gave rise to no gratitude in shareholding
hearts; it seemed merely to render them the more
furious. The baser passions had been let loose in the
Cannon Street Hotel. The directors had possibly been
expecting the baser passions, for a posse of policemen
was handy at the door, and one shareholder, to save
him from having the blood of Marquises on his soul,
was ejected. Ultimately, according to the picturesque
phrases of the *Financial Times* report, the meeting
broke up in confusion.

"How much have you got in Cohoon's?" Priam
asked Alice, after they had looked through the report
together.

"All I have is in Cohoon's," said she, "except this
house. Father left me it like that. He always said
there was nothing like a brewery. I've heard him say
many and many a time a brewery was better than con-
sols. I think there's 200 £5 shares. Yes, that's it.
But of course they're worth much more than that.
They're worth about £12 each. All I know is they

bring me in £150 a year as regular as the clock. What's that there, after 'broke up in confusion?'"

She pointed with her finger to a paragraph, and he read in a low voice the fluctuations of Cohoon's Ordinary Shares during the afternoon.   They had finished at £6 5s. Mrs. Henry Leek had lost over £1,000 in about half-a-day.

"They've always brought me in £150 a year," she insisted, as though she had been saying: "It's always been Christmas Day on the 25th of December, and of course it will be the same this year."

"It doesn't look as if they'd bring you in anything this time," said he.

"Oh, but Henry!" she protested.

Beer had failed! That was the truth of it. Beer had failed. Who would have guessed that beer could fail in England? The wisest, the most prudent men in Lombard Street had put their trust in beer, as the last grand bulwark of the nation; and even beer had failed. The foundations of England's greatness were, if not gone, going. Insufficient to argue bad management, indiscreet purchases of licences at inflated prices! In the excellent old days a brewery would stand an indefinite amount of bad management! Times were changed. The British workman, caught in a wave of temperance, could no longer be relied upon to drink! It was the crown of his sins against society. Trade unions were nothing

to this latest caprice of his, which spread desolation in
a thousand genteel homes.   Alice wondered what her
father would have said, had he lived.   On the whole,
she was glad that he did not happen to be alive.   The
shock to him would have been too rude.   The floor
seemed to be giving way under Alice, melting into a
sort of bog that would swallow up her and her husband.
For years, without any precise information, but merely
by instinct, she had felt that England, beneath the sur-
face, was not quite the island it had been—and here
was the awful proof.

She gazed at her husband, as a wife ought to gaze
at her husband in a crisis.   His thoughts were much
vaguer than hers, his thoughts about money being always extremely vague.

"Suppose you went up to the City and saw Mr.
What's-his-name?" she suggested, meaning the signatory
of the letter.

"*Me!*"

It was a cry of the soul aghast, a cry drawn out of
him sharply, by a most genuine cruel alarm.   Him to
go up to the City to interview a solicitor!   Why, the
poor dear woman must be demented!   He could not
have done it for a million pounds.   The thought of it
made him sick, raising the whole of his lunch to his
throat, as by some sinister magic.

She saw and translated the look on his face.   It was

a look of horror. And at once she made excuses for
him to herself. At once she said to herself that it was
no use pretending that her Henry was like other men.
He was not. He was a dreamer. He was, at times,
amazingly peculiar. But he was her Henry. In any
other man than her Henry a hesitation to take charge
of his wife's financial affairs would have been ridiculous;
it would have been effeminate. But Henry was Henry.
She was gradually learning that truth. He was adorable;
but he was Henry. With magnificent strength of mind
she collected herself.

"No," she said cheerfully. "As they're my shares,
perhaps I'd better go. Unless we *both* go!" She encountered his eye again, and added quietly: "No, I'll
go alone."

He sighed his relief. He could not help sighing his
relief.

And, after meticulously washing-up and straighten-
ing, she departed, and Priam remained solitary with his
ideas about married life and the fiscal question.

Alice was assuredly the very mirror of discretion.
Never, since that unanswered query as to savings at the
Grand Babylon, had she subjected him to any inquisi-
tion concerning money. Never had she talked of her
own means, save in casual phrase now and then to
assure him that there was enough. She had indeed
refused banknotes diffidently offered to her by him,

telling him to keep them by him till need of them arose. Never had she discoursed of her own past life, nor led him on to discourse of his.   She was one of those women for whom neither the past nor the future seems to exist—they are always so occupied with the important present.   He and she had both of them relied on their judgment of character as regarded each other's worthiness and trustworthiness.   And he was the last man in the world to be a chancellor of the exchequer.   To him, money was a quite uninteresting token that had to pass through your hands.   He had always had enough of it. He had always had too much of it.   Even at Putney he had had too much of it.   The better part of Henry Leek's two hundred pounds had remained in his pockets, and under his own will he had his pound a week, of which he never spent more than a few shillings.   His distractions were tobacco (which cost him about twopence a day), walking about and enjoying colour effects and the oddities of the streets (which cost him nearly nought), and reading: there were three shops of Putney where all that is greatest in literature could be bought for fourpence-halfpenny a volume.   Do what he could, he could not read away more than ninepence a week. He was positively accumulating money.   You may say that he ought to have compelled Alice to accept money. The idea never occurred to him.   In his scheme of things money had not been a matter of sufficient urgency to necessitate an argument with one's wife. She was always welcome to all that he had.

And now suddenly, money acquired urgency in his eyes. It was most disturbing. He was not frightened: he was merely disturbed. If he had ever known the sensation of wanting money and not being able to obtain it, he would probably have been frightened. But this sensation was unfamiliar to him. Not once in his whole career had he hesitated to change gold from fear that the end of gold was at hand.

All kinds of problems crowded round him.

He went out for a stroll to escape the problems. But they accompanied him. He walked through exactly the same streets as had delighted him in the morning. And they had ceased to delight him. This surely could not be ideal Putney that he was in! It must be some other place of the same name. The mismanagement of a brewery a hundred and fifty miles from London; the failure of the British working-man to drink his customary pints in several scattered scores of public-houses, had most unaccountably knocked the bottom out of the Putney system of practical philosophy. Putney posters were now merely disgusting, Putney trade gross and futile, the tobacconist a narrow-minded and stupid bourgeois; and so on.

Alice and he met on their doorstep, each in the act of pulling out a latchkey.

"Oh!" she said, when they were inside, "it's done for! There's no mistake—it's done for! We sha'n't get a penny this year, not one penny! And he doesn't think there'll be anything next year either! And the shares 'll go down yet, he says. I never heard of such a thing in all my life! Did you?"

He admitted sympathetically that he had not.

After she had been upstairs and come down again her mood suddenly changed. "Well," she smiled, "whether we get anything or not, it's tea-time. So we'll have tea. I've no patience with worrying. I said I should make pastry after tea, and I will too. See if I don't!"

The tea was perhaps slightly more elaborate than usual.

After tea he heard her singing in the kitchen. And he was moved to go and look at her. There she was, with her sleeves turned back, and a large pinafore apron over her rich bosom, kneading flour. He would have liked to approach her and kiss her. But he never could accomplish feats of that kind at unusual moments.

"Oh!" she laughed. "You can look! *I'm* not worrying. I've no patience with worrying."

Later in the afternoon he went out; rather like a person who has reasons for leaving inconspicuously. He had made a great, a critical resolve. He passed furtively down Werter Road into the High Street, and then stood a moment outside Stawley's stationery shop, which is also a library, an emporium of leather-bags, and an artists'-colourman's. He entered Stawley's blushing, trembling—he a man of fifty who could not see his own toes—and asked for certain tubes of colour. An energetic young lady who seemed to know all about the graphic arts endeavoured to sell to him a magnificent and complicated box of paints, which opened out into an easel and a stool, and contained a palette of a shape preferred by the late Edwin Long, R.A., a selection of colours which had been approved by the late Lord Leighton, P.R.A., and a patent drying-oil which (she said) had been used by Whistler. Priam Farll got away from the shop without this apparatus for the confection of masterpieces, but he did not get away without a sketching-box which he had had no intention of buying. The young lady was too energetic for him. He was afraid of being too curt with her lest she should turn on him and tell him that pretence was useless— she knew he was Priam Farll. He felt guilty, and he felt that he looked guilty. As he hurried along the High Street towards the river with the paint-box it appeared to him that policemen observed him inimically and cocked their helmets at him, as who should say: "See here; this won't do. You're supposed to be in Westminster Abbey. You'll be locked up if you're too brazen."

The tide was out. He sneaked down to the gravelly shore a little above the steamer pier, and hid himself between the piles, glancing around him in a scared fashion. He might have been about to commit a crime. Then he opened the sketch-box, and oiled the palette, and tried the elasticity of the brushes on his hand. And he made a sketch of the scene before him. He did it very quickly—in less than half-an-hour. He had made thousands of such colour "notes" in his life, and he would never part with any of them. He had always hated to part with his notes. Doubtless his cousin Duncan had them now, if Duncan had discovered his address in Paris, as Duncan probably had.

When it was finished, he inspected the sketch, half shutting his eyes and holding it about three feet off. It was good. Except for a few pencil scrawls done in sheer absent-mindedness and hastily destroyed, this was the first sketch he had made since the death of Henry Leek. But it was very good. "No mistake who's done that!" he murmured; and added: "That's the devil of it. Any expert would twig it in a minute. There's only one man that could have done it. I shall have to do something worse than that!" He shut up the box and with a bang as an amative couple came into sight. He need not have done so, for the couple vanished instantly in deep disgust at being robbed of their retreat between the piles.

Alice was nearing the completion of pastry when he returned in the dusk; he smelt the delicious proof. Creeping quietly upstairs, he deposited his brushes in an empty attic at the top of the house.   Then he washed his hands with especial care to remove all odour of paint.   And at dinner he endeavoured to put on the mien of innocence.

She was cheerful, but it was the cheerfulness of determined effort.   They naturally talked of the situation.   It appeared that she had a reserve of money in the bank—as much as would suffice her for quite six months.   He told her with false buoyancy that there need never be the slightest difficulty as to money; he had money, and he could always earn more.

"If you think I'm going to let you go into another situation," she said, "you're mistaken.   That's all."   And her lips were firm.

This staggered him.   He never could remember for more than half-an-hour at a time that he was a retired valet.   And it was decidedly not her practice to remind him of the fact.   The notion of himself in a situation as valet was half ridiculous and half tragical.   He could no more be a valet than he could be a stockbroker or a wire-walker.

"I wasn't thinking of that," he stammered.

"Then what were you thinking of?" she asked.

"Oh! I don't know!" he said vaguely.

"Because those things they advertise—home-work, envelope addressing, or selling gramophones on commission—they're no good, you know!"

He shuddered.

The next morning he bought a 36 × 24 canvas, and more brushes and tubes, and surreptitiously introduced them into the attic. Happily it was the charwoman's day and Alice was busy enough to ignore him. With an old table and the tray out of a travelling-trunk, he arranged a substitute for an easel, and began to try to paint a bad picture from his sketch. But in a quarter of an hour he discovered that he was exactly as fitted to paint a bad picture as to be a valet. He could not sentimentalise the tones, nor falsify the values. He simply could not; the attempt to do so annoyed him. All men are capable of stooping beneath their highest selves, and in several directions Priam Farll could have stooped. But not on canvas! He could only produce his best. He could only render nature as he saw nature. And it was instinct, rather than conscience, that prevented him from stooping.

In three days, during which he kept Alice out of the attic partly by lies and partly by locking the door, the picture was finished; and he had forgotten all about everything except his profession. He had become a different man, a very excited man.

"By Jove," he exclaimed, surveying the picture, "I can paint!"

Artists do occasionally soliloquise in this way.

The picture was dazzling! What atmosphere! What poetry! And what profound fidelity to nature's facts! It was precisely such a picture as he was in the habit of selling for £800 or a £1,000, before his burial in Westminster Abbey! Indeed, the trouble was that it had "Priam Farll" written all over it, just as the sketch had!

CHAPTER VII.

THE CONFESSION.

THAT evening he was very excited, and he seemed to take no thought to disguise his excitement. The fact was, he could not have disguised it, even if he had tried. The fever of artistic creation was upon him— all the old desires and the old exhausting joys. His genius had been lying idle, like a lion in a thicket, and now it had sprung forth ravening. For months he had not handled a brush; for months his mind had deliberately avoided the question of painting, being content with the observation only of beauty. A week ago, if he had deliberately asked himself whether he would ever paint again, he might have answered, "Perhaps not." Such is man's ignorance of his own nature! And now the lion of his genius was standing over him, its paw on his breast, and making a great noise.

He saw that the last few months had been merely an interlude, that he would be forced to paint—or go mad; and that nothing else mattered. He saw also that he could only paint in one way—Priam Farll's way. If it was discovered that Priam Farll was not buried in Westminster Abbey; if there was a scandal, and legal unpleasantness—well, so much the worse! But he must paint.

Not for money, mind you! Incidentally, of course, he would earn money. But he had already quite forgotten that life has its financial aspect.

So in the sitting-room in Werter Road, he walked uneasily to and fro, squeezing between the table and the sideboard, and then skirting the fireplace where Alice sat with a darning apparatus upon her knees, and her spectacles on—she wore spectacles when she had to look fixedly at very dark objects. The room was ugly in a pleasant Putneyish way, with a couple of engravings after B. W. Leader, R.A., a too realistic wall-paper, hot brown furniture with ribbed legs, a carpet with the characteristics of a retired governess who has taken to drink, and a black cloud on the ceiling over the incandescent burners. Happily these surroundings did not annoy him. They did not annoy him because he never saw them. When his eyes were not resting on beautiful things, they were not in this world of reality at all. His sole idea about house-furnishing was an easy-chair.

"Harry," said his wife, "don't you think you'd better sit down?"

The calm voice of commonsense stopped him in his circular tour. He glanced at Alice, and she, removing

10*

her spectacles, glanced at him. The seal on his watch-chain dangled free. He had to talk to someone, and his wife was there—not only the most convenient but the most proper person to talk to. A tremendous impulse seized him to tell her everything; she would understand; she always did understand; and she never allowed herself to be startled. The most singular occurrences, immediately they touched her, were somehow transformed into credible daily, customary events. Thus the disaster of the brewery! She had accepted it as though the ruins of breweries were a spectacle to be witnessed at every street-corner.

Yes, he should tell her. Three minutes ago he had no intention of telling her, or anyone, anything. He decided in an instant. To tell her his secret would lead up naturally to the picture which he had just finished.

"I say, Alice," he said, "I want to talk to you."

"Well," she said, "I wish you'd talk to me sitting down. I don't know what's come over you this last day or two."

He sat down. He did not feel really intimate with her at that moment. And their marriage seemed to him, in a way, artificial, scarcely a fact. He did not know that it takes years to accomplish full intimacy between husband and wife.

"You know," he said, "Henry Leek isn't my real name."

"Oh, isn't it?" she said. "What does that matter?"

She was not in the least surprised to hear that Henry Leek was not his real name. She was a wise woman, and knew the strangeness of the world. And she had married him simply because he was himself, because he existed in a particular manner (whose charm for her she could not have described) from hour to hour.

"So long as you haven't committed a murder or anything," she added, with her tranquil smile.

"My real name is Priam Farll," he said gruffly. The gruffness was caused by timidity.

"I thought Priam Farll was your gentleman's name."

"To tell you the truth," he said nervously, "there was a mistake. That photograph that was sent to you was my photograph."

"Yes," she said. "I know it was. And what of it?"

"I mean," he blundered on, "it was my valet that died—not me. You see, the doctor, when he came, thought that Leek was me, and I didn't tell him differently, because I was afraid of all the bother. I just let it slide—and there were other reasons. You know how I am . . ."

"I don't know what you're talking about," she said.

"Can't you understand? It's simple enough. I'm Priam Farll, and I had a valet named Henry Leek, and he died, and they thought it was me. Only it wasn't."

He saw her face change and then compose itself.

"Then it's this Henry Leek that is buried in West-minster Abbey, instead of you?" Her voice was very soft and soothing. And the astonishing woman resumed her spectacles and her long needle.

"Yes, of course."

Here he burst into the whole story, into the middle of it, continuing to the end, and then going back to the commencement. He left out nothing, and nobody, ex-cept Lady Sophia Entwistle.

"I see," she observed. "And you've never said a word?"

"Not a word."

"If I were you I should still keep perfectly silent about it," she almost whispered persuasively. "It'll be just as well. If I were you, I shouldn't worry myself. I can quite understand how it happened, and I'm glad you've told me. But don't worry. You've been exciting yourself these last two or three days. I thought it was about my money business, but I see it wasn't. At least that may have brought it on, like. Now the best thing you can do is to forget it."

She did not believe him! She simply discredited the whole story; and, told in Werter Road, like that, the story did sound fantastic; it did come very near to passing belief. She had always noticed a certain queerness in her husband. His sudden gaieties about a tint in the sky or the gesture of a horse in the street, for example, were most uncanny. And he had peculiar absences of mind that she could never account for. She was sure that he must have been a very bad valet. However, she did not marry him for a valet, but for a husband; and she was satisfied with her bargain. What if he did suffer under a delusion? The exposure of that delusion merely crystallised into a definite shape her vague suspicions concerning his mentality. Besides, it was a harmless delusion. And it explained things. It explained, among other things, why he had gone to stay at the Grand Babylon Hotel. That must have been the inception of the delusion. She was glad to know the worst.

She adored him more than ever.

There was a silence.

"No," she repeated, in the most matter-of-fact tone, "I should say nothing, in your place. I should forget it."

"You would?" He drummed on the table.

"I should! And whatever you do, don't worry." Her accents were the coaxing accents of a nurse with a child—or with a lunatic.

He perceived now with the utmost clearness that she did not believe a word of what he had said, and that in her magnificent and calm sagacity she was only

trying to humour him. He had expected to disturb her
soul to its profoundest depths; he had expected that
they would sit up half the night discussing the situation.
And lo!—"I should forget it," indulgently! And a mild
continuance of darning!

He had to think, and think hard.

TEARS.

"Henry," she called out the next morning, as he
disappeared up the stairs. "What *are* you doing up
there?"

She had behaved exactly as if nothing had happened;
and she was one of those women whose prudent policy
it is to let their men alone even to the furthest limit of
patience; but she had nerves, too, and they were being
affected. For three days Henry had really been too
mysterious!

He stopped, and put his head over the banisters,
and in a queer, moved voice answered:

"Come and see."

Sooner or later she must see. Sooner or later the
already distended situation must get more and more
distended until it burst with a loud report. Let the
moment be sooner, he swiftly decided.

So she went and saw.

Half-way up the attic stairs she began to sniff, and

as he turned the knob of the attic door for her she said, "What a smell of paint! I fancied yesterday——"

If she had been clever enough she would have said, "What a smell of masterpieces!" But her cleverness lay in other fields.

"You surely haven't been aspinalling that bath-room chair? . . . Oh!"

This loud exclamation escaped from her as she entered the attic and saw the back of the picture which Priam had lodged on the said bath-room chair—filched by him from the bath-room on the previous day. She stepped to the vicinity of the window and obtained a good view of the picture. It was brilliantly shining in the light of morn. It looked glorious; it was a fit companion of many pictures from the same hand distributed among European galleries. It had that priceless quality, at once noble and radiant, which distinguished all Priam's work. It transformed the attic; and thousands of amateurs and students, from St. Petersburg to San Francisco, would have gone into that attic with their hats off and a thrill in the spine, had they known what was there and had they been invited to enter and worship. Priam himself was pleased; he was delighted; he was enthusiastic. And he stood near the picture, glancing at it and then glancing at Alice, nervously, like a mother whose sister-in-law has come to look at the baby. As for Alice, she said nothing. She had first of all to take in the fact that her husband had been ungenerous enough to keep her quite in the dark as to the nature of his secret activities; then she had to take in the fact of the picture.

"Did you do that?" she said limply.

"Yes," said he, with all the casualness that he could assume. "How does it strike you?" And to himself: "This'll make her see I'm not a mere lunatic. This'll give her a shaking up."

"I'm sure it's beautiful," she said kindly, but without the slightest conviction. "What is it? Is that Putney Bridge?"

"Yes," he said.

"I thought it was. I thought it must be. Well, I never knew you could paint. It's beautiful—for an amateur." She said this firmly and yet endearingly, and met his eyes with her eyes. It was her tactful method of politely causing him to see that she had not accepted last night's yarn very seriously. His eyes fell, not hers.

"No, no, no!" he expostulated with quick vivacity, as she stepped towards the canvas. "Don't come any nearer. You're at just the right distance."

"Oh! If you don't *want* me to see it close," she humoured him. "What a pity you haven't put an omnibus on the bridge!"

"There is one," said he. "*That's* one." He pointed.

"Oh yes! Yes, I see. But, you know, I think it looks rather more like a Carter Paterson van than an omnibus. If you could paint some letters on it—'Union Jack' or 'Vanguard,' then people would be sure. But it's beautiful. I suppose you learnt to paint from your——" She checked herself. "What's that red streak behind?"

"That's the railway bridge," he muttered.

"Oh, of course it is! How silly of me! Now if you were to put a train on that. The worst of trains in pictures is that they never seem to be going along. I've noticed that on the sides of furniture vans, haven't you? But if you put a signal against it, then people would understand that the train had stopped. I'm not sure whether there *is* a signal on the bridge though."

He made no remark.

"And I see that's the Elk public-house there on the right. You've just managed to get it in. I can recognise that quite easily. Anyone would."

He still made no remark.

"What are you going to do with it?" she asked gently.

"Going to sell it, my dear," he replied grimly. "It may surprise you to know that that canvas is worth at the very least £800. There would be a devil of a row and rumpus in Bond Street and elsewhere if they knew I was painting here instead of rotting in Westminster

Abbey. I don't propose to sign it—I seldom did sign
my pictures—and we shall see what we shall see. . . .
I've got fifteen hundred for little things not so good as
that. I'll let it go for what it'll fetch. We shall soon
be wanting money."

The tears rose to Alice's eyes. She saw that he
was infinitely more mad than she imagined—with his
£800 and his £1,500 for daubs of pictures that conveyed no meaning whatever to the eye! Why, you
could purchase real, professional pictures, of lakes and
mountains, exquisitely finished, at the frame-makers in
High Street for three pounds apiece! And here he
was rambling in hundreds and thousands! She saw
that that extraordinary notion about being able to paint
was a natural consequence of the pathetic delusion to
which he had given utterance yesterday. And she
wondered what would follow next. Who could have
guessed that the seeds of lunacy were in such a man?
Yes, harmless lunacy, but lunacy nevertheless! She
distinctly remembered the little shock with which she
had learned that he was staying at the Grand Babylon
on his own account, as a wealthy visitor. She thought it
bizarre, but she certainly had not taken it for a sign of
lunacy. And yet it had been a sign of madness. And
the worst of harmless lunacy was that it might develop
at any moment into harmful lunacy.

There was one thing to do, and only one: keep

him quiet, shield him from all troubles and alarms. It was disturbance of spirit which induced these mental derangements. His master's death had upset him. And now he had been upset by her disgraceful brewery company.

She made a step towards him, and then hesitated. She had to form a plan of campaign all in a moment! She had to keep her wits and to use them! How could she give him confidence about his absurd picture? She noticed that naïve look that sometimes came into his eyes, a boyish expression that gave the lie to his greying beard and his generous proportions.

He laughed, until, as she came closer, he saw the tears on her eyelids. Then he ceased laughing. She fingered the edge of his coat, cajolingly.

"It's a beautiful picture!" she repeated again and again. "And if you like I will see if I can sell it for you. But, Henry——"

"Well?"

"Please, please don't bother about money. We shall have *heaps.* There's no occasion for you to bother, and I won't *have* you bothering."

"What are you crying for?" he asked in a murmur.

"It's only—only because I think it's so nice of you trying to earn money like that," she lied. "I'm not really crying."

And she ran away, downstairs, really crying. It

was excessively comic, but he had better not follow her, lest he might cry too. . . .

A PATRON OF THE ARTS.

A lull followed this crisis in the affairs of No. 29 Werter Road. Priam went on painting, and there was now no need for secrecy about it. But his painting was not made a subject of conversation. Both of them hesitated to touch it, she from tact, and he because her views on the art seemed to him to be lacking in subtlety. In every marriage there is a topic—there are usually several—which the husband will never broach to the wife, out of respect for his respect for her. Priam scarcely guessed that Alice imagined him to be on the way to lunacy. He thought she merely thought him queer, as artists *are* queer to non-artists. And he was accustomed to that; Henry Leek had always thought him queer. As for Alice's incredulous attitude towards the revelation of his identity, he did not mentally accuse her of treating him as either a liar or a madman. On reflection he persuaded himself that she regarded the story as a bad joke, as one of his impulsive, capricious essays in the absurd.

Thus the march of evolution was apparently arrested in Werter Road during three whole days. And then a singular event happened, and progress was

resumed. Priam had been out since early morning on
the riverside, sketching, and had reached Barnes, from
which town he returned over Barnes Common, and so
by the Upper Richmond Road to High Street. He was
on the south side of Upper Richmond Road, whereas
his tobacconist's shop was on the north side, near the
corner. An unfamiliar peculiarity of the shop caused
him to cross the street, for he was not in want of
tobacco. It was the look of the window that drew
him. He stopped on the refuge in the centre of the
street. There was no necessity to go further. His
picture of Putney Bridge was in the middle of the
window. He stared at it fixedly. He believed his
eyes, for his eyes were the finest part of him and never
deceived him; but perhaps if he had been a person
with ordinary eyes he would scarce have been able to
believe them. The canvas was indubitably there present
in the window. It had been put in a cheap frame such
as is used for chromographic advertisements of ships,
soups, and tobacco. He was almost sure that he had
seen that same frame, within the shop, round a pictorial
announcement of Taddy's Snuff. The tobacconist had
probably removed the eighteenth-century aristocrat with
his fingers to his nose, from the frame, and replaced
him with Putney Bridge. In any event the frame was
about half-an-inch too long for the canvas, but the gap
was scarcely observable. On the frame was a large

notice, 'For sale.' And around it were the cigars of two hemispheres, from Syak Whiffs at a penny each to precious Murias; and cigarettes of every allurement; and the multitudinous fragments of all advertised tobaccos; and meerschaums and briars, and patent pipes and diagrams of their secret machinery; and cigarette- and cigar-holders laid on plush; and pocket receptacles in aluminium and other precious metals.

Shining there, the picture had a most incongruous appearance. He blushed as he stood on the refuge. It seemed to him that the mere incongruity of the spectacle must inevitably attract crowds, gradually blocking the street, and that when some individual not absolutely a fool in art, had perceived the quality of the picture—well, then the trouble of public curiosity and of journalistic inquisitiveness would begin. He wondered that he could ever have dreamed of concealing his identity on a canvas. The thing simply shouted "Priam Farll," every inch of it. In any exhibition of pictures in London, Paris, Rome, Milan, Munich, New York or Boston, it would have been the cynosure, the target of ecstatic admirations. It was just such another work as his celebrated "Pont d'Austerlitz," which hung in the Luxembourg. And neither a frame of "chemical gold," nor the extremely variegated coloration of the other merchandise on sale could kill it.

However, there were no signs of a crowd. People

passed to and fro, just as though there had not been a masterpiece within ten thousand miles of them. Once a servant girl, a loaf of bread in her red arms, stopped to glance at the window, but in an instant she was gone, running.

Priam's first instinctive movement had been to plunge into the shop, and demand from his tobacconist an explanation of the phenomenon. But of course he checked himself. Of course he knew that the presence of his picture in the window could only be due to the enterprise of Alice.

He went slowly home.

The sound of his latchkey in the keyhole brought her into the hall ere he had opened the door.

"Oh, Henry," she said—she was quite excited—"I must tell you. I was passing Mr. Aylmer's this morning just as he was dressing his window, and the thought struck me that he might put your picture in. So I ran in and asked him. He said he would if he could have it at once. So I came and got it. He found a frame, and wrote out a ticket, and asked after you. No one could have been kinder. You must go and have a look at it. I shouldn't be at all surprised if it gets sold like that."

Priam answered nothing for a moment. He could not.

"What did Aylmer say about it?" he asked.

"Oh!" said his wife quickly, "you can't expect Mr.

Aylmer to understand these things. It's not in his line. But he was glad to oblige us. I saw that he arranged it nicely."

"Well," said Priam discreetly, "that's all right. Suppose we have lunch?"

Curious—her relations with Mr. Aylmer! It was she who had recommended him to go to Mr. Aylmer's when, on the first morning of his residence in Putney, he had demanded, "Any decent tobacconists in this happy region?" He suspected that, had it not been for Aylmer's bedridden and incurable wife, Alice's name might have been Aylmer. He suspected Aylmer of a hopeless passion for Alice. He was glad that Alice had not been thrown away on Aylmer. He could not imagine himself now without Alice. In spite of her ideas on the graphic arts, Alice was his air, his atmosphere, his oxygen; and also his umbrella to shield him from the hail of untoward circumstances. Curious—the process of love! It was the power of love that had put that picture in the tobacconist's window.

Whatever power had put it there, no power seemed strong enough to get it out again. It lay exposed in the window for weeks and never drew a crowd, nor caused a sensation of any kind! Not a word in the newspapers! London, the acknowledged art-centre of the world, calmly went its ways. The sole immediate result was that Priam changed his tobacconist, and the direction of his promenades.

At last another singular event happened.

Alice beamingly put five sovereigns into Priam's hand one evening.

"It's been sold for five guineas," she said, joyous. "Mr. Aylmer didn't want to keep anything for himself, but I insisted on his having the odd shillings. I think it's splendid, simply splendid! Of course I always *did* think it was a beautiful picture," she added.

The fact was that this astounding sale for so large a sum as five pounds, of a picture done in the attic by her Henry, had enlarged her ideas of Henry's skill. She could no longer regard his painting as the caprice of a gentle lunatic. There was something *in* it. And now she wanted to persuade herself that she had known from the first there was something in it.

The picture had been bought by the eccentric and notorious landlord of the Elk Hotel, down by the river, on a Sunday afternoon when he was—not drunk, but more optimistic than the state of English society warrants. He liked the picture because his public-house was so unmistakably plain in it. He ordered a massive gold frame for it, and hung it in his saloon-bar. His career as a patron of the arts was unfortunately cut short by an order signed by his doctors for his incarceration in a lunatic asylum. All Putney had been saying for years that he would end in the asylum, and all Putney was right.

11*

CHAPTER VIII.

AN INVASION.

ONE afternoon, in December, Priam and Alice were in the sitting-room together, and Alice was about to prepare tea. The drawn-thread cloth was laid diagonally on the table (because Alice had seen cloths so laid on model tea-tables in model rooms at Waring's), the strawberry jam occupied the northern point of the compass, and the marmalade was antarctic, while brittle cakes and spongy cakes represented the occident and the orient respectively. Bread-and-butter stood, rightly, for the centre of the universe. Silver ornamented the spread, and Alice's two tea-pots (for she would never allow even Chinese tea to remain on the leaves for more than five minutes) and Alice's water-jug with the patent balanced lid, occupied a tray off the cloth. At some distance, but still on the table, a kettle moaned over a spirit-lamp. Alice was cutting bread for toast. The fire was of the right redness for toast, and a toasting-fork lay handy. As winter advanced, Alice's teas had a tendency to become cosier and cosier, and also more luxurious, more of a ritualistic ceremony. And to avoid the trouble and danger of going through a cold passage to the kitchen, she arranged matters so that the entire operation could be performed with comfort and decency in the sitting-room itself.

Priam was rolling cigarettes, many of them, and placing them, as he rolled them, in order on the mantelpiece. A happy, mild couple! And a couple, one would judge from the richness of the tea, with no immediate need of money. Over two years, however, had passed since the catastrophe to Cohoon's, and Cohoon's had in no way recovered therefrom. Yet money had been regularly found for the household. The manner of its finding was soon to assume importance in the careers of Priam and Alice. But, ere that moment, an astonishing and vivid experience happened to them. One might have supposed that, in the life of Priam Farll at least, enough of the astonishing and the vivid had already happened. Nevertheless, what had already happened was as customary and unexciting as addressing envelopes, compared to the next event.

The next event began at the instant when Alice was sticking the long fork into a round of bread. There was a knock at the front door, a knock formidable and reverberating, the knock of fate, perhaps, but fate disguised as a coalheaver.

Alice answered it. She always answered knocks; Priam never. She shielded him from every rough or

unexpected contact, just as his valet used to do.   The
gas in the hall was not lighted, and so she stopped to
light it, darkness having fallen.   Then she opened the
door, and saw, in the gloom, a short, thin woman
standing on the step, a woman of advanced middle-age,
dressed with a kind of shabby neatness.   It seemed
impossible that so frail and unimportant a creature
could have made such a noise on the door.

"Is this Mr. Henry Leek's?" asked the visitor, in a
dissatisfied, rather weary tone.

"Yes," said Alice.   Which was not quite true.
"This" was assuredly hers, rather than her husband's.

"Oh!" said the woman, glancing behind her; and
entered nervously, without invitation.

At the same moment three male figures sprang, or
rushed, out of the strip of front garden, and followed
the woman into the hall, lunging up against Alice, and
breathing loudly.   One of the trio was a strong, heavy-
faced, heavy-handed, louring man of some thirty years
(it seemed probable that he was the knocker), and the
others were curates, with the proper physical attributes
of curates; that is to say, they were of ascetic habit and
clean-shaven and had ingenuous eyes.

The hall now appeared like the antechamber of a
May-meeting, and as Alice had never seen it so peopled
before, she vented a natural exclamation of surprise.

"Yes," said one of the curates, fiercely.   "You may

say 'Lord,' but we were determined to get in, and in we have got. John, shut the door. Mother, don't put yourself about."

John, being the heavy-faced and heavy-handed man, shut the door.

"Where is Mr. Henry Leek?" demanded the other curate.

Now Priam, whose curiosity had been excusably excited by the unusual sounds in the hall, was peeping through a chink of the sitting-room door, and the elderly woman caught the glint of his eyes. She pushed open the door, and, after a few seconds' inspection of him, said:

"There you are, Henry! After thirty years! To think of it!"

Priam was utterly at a loss.

"I'm his wife, ma'am," the visitor continued sadly to Alice. "I'm sorry to have to tell you. I'm his wife. I'm the rightful Mrs. Henry Leek, and these are my sons, come with me to see that I get justice."

Alice recovered very quickly from the shock of amazement. She was a woman not easily to be startled by the vagaries of human nature. She had often heard of bigamy, and that her husband should prove to be a bigamist did not throw her into a swoon. She at once, in her own mind, began to make excuses for him. She said to herself, as she inspected the real Mrs. Henry

Leek, that the real Mrs. Henry Leek had certainly the temperament which manufactures bigamists. She understood how a person may slide into bigamy. And after thirty years! . . . She never thought of bigamy as a crime, nor did it occur to her to run out and drown herself for shame because she was not properly married to Priam!

No, it has to be said in favour of Alice that she invariably took things as they were.

"I think you'd better all come in and sit down quietly," she said.

"Eh! It's very kind of you," said the mother of the curates, limply.

The last thing that the curates wanted to do was to sit down quietly. But they had to sit down. Alice made them sit side by side on the sofa. The heavy, elder brother, who had not spoken a word, sat on a chair between the sideboard and the door. Their mother sat on a chair near the table. Priam fell into his easy-chair between the fireplace and the sideboard. As for Alice, she remained standing; she showed no nervousness except in her handling of the toasting-fork.

It was a great situation. But unfortunately ordinary people are so unaccustomed to the great situation, that, when it chances to come, they feel themselves incapable of living up to it. A person gazing in at the window, and unacquainted with the facts, might have guessed that the affair was simply a tea-party at which the guests had arrived a little too soon and where no one was startlingly proficient in the art of small-talk.

Still, the curates were apparently bent on doing their best.

"Now, mother!" one of them urged her.

The mother, as if a spring had been touched in her, began: "He married me just thirty years ago, ma'am; and four months after my eldest was born— that's John there" (pointing to the corner near the door)—"he just walked out of the house and left me. I'm sorry to have to say it. Yes, sorry I am! But there it is. And never a word had I ever given him! And eight months after that my twins were born. That's Harry and Matthew"—(pointing to the sofa)— "Harry I called after his father because I thought he was like him, and just to show I bore no ill-feeling, and hoping he'd come back! And there I was with these little children! And not a word of explanation did I ever have. I heard of Harry five years later— when Johnnie was nearly five—but he was on the Continent and I couldn't go trapesing about with three babies. Besides, if I *had* gone! . . . Sorry I am to say it, ma'am; but many's the time he's beaten me, yes, with his hands and his fists! He's knocked me about above a bit. And I never gave him a word back. He was my husband, for better for worse, and I forgave him and I still do. Forgive and forget, that's what I say. We only heard of him through Matthew being second curate at St. Paul's, and in charge of the mission hall. It was your milkman that happened to tell Matthew that he had a customer same name as himself. And you know how one thing leads to another. So we're here!"

"I never saw this lady in my life," said Priam excitedly, "and I'm absolutely certain I never married her. I never married anyone; except, of course, you, Alice!"

"Then how do you explain this, sir?" exclaimed Matthew, the younger twin, jumping up and taking a blue paper from his pocket. "Be so good as to pass this to father," he said, handing the paper to Alice.

Alice inspected the document. It was a certificate of the marriage of Henry Leek, valet, and Sarah Featherstone, spinster, at a registry office in Paddington. Priam also inspected it. This was one of Leek's escapades! No revelations as to the past of Henry Leek would have surprised him. There was nothing to be done except to give a truthful denial of identity and to persist in that denial. Useless to say soothingly to the lady visitor that she was the widow of a gentleman who had been laid to rest in Westminster Abbey!

"I know nothing about it," said Priam doggedly.

"I suppose you'll not deny, sir, that your name is

Henry Leek," said Henry, jumping up to stand by
Matthew.

"I deny everything," said Priam doggedly. How
could he explain? If he had not been able to convince
Alice that he was not Henry Leek, could he hope to
convince these visitors?

"I suppose, madam," Henry continued, addressing
Alice in impressive tones as if she were a crowded
congregation, "that at any rate you and my father are
—er—living here together under the name of Mr. and
Mrs. Henry Leek?"

Alice merely lifted her eyebrows.

"It's all a mistake," said Priam impatiently. Then
he had a brilliant inspiration. "As if there was only
one Henry Leek in the world!"

"Do you really recognise my husband?" Alice
asked.

"Your husband, madam!" Matthew protested,
shocked.

"I wouldn't say that I recognised him as he *was,*"
said the real Mrs. Henry Leek. "No more than he re-
cognises me. After thirty years! . . . Last time I saw
him he was only twenty-two or twenty-three. But he's
the same sort of man, and he has the same eyes. And
look at Henry's eyes. Besides, I heard twenty-five
years ago that he'd gone into service with a Mr. Priam
Farll, a painter or something, him that was buried in

Westminster Abbey.   And everybody in Putney knows
that this gentleman——"

"Gentleman!" murmured Matthew, discontented.

"Was valet to Mr. Priam Farll.   We've heard that
everywhere."

"I suppose you'll not deny," said Henry the younger,
"that Priam Farll wouldn't be likely to have *two* valets
named Henry Leek?"

Crushed by this Socratic reasoning, Priam kept
silence, nursing his knees and staring into the fire.

Alice went to the sideboard where she kept her
best china, and took out three extra cups and saucers.

"I think we'd all better have some tea," she said
tranquilly.   And then she got the tea-caddy and put
seven teaspoonfuls of tea into one of the tea-pots.

"It's very kind of you, I'm sure," whimpered the
authentic Mrs. Henry Leek.

"Now, mother, don't give way!" the curates ad-
monished her.

"Don't you remember, Henry," she went on whim-
pering to Priam, "how you said you wouldn't be married in a church, not for anybody?   And how I gave
way to you, like I always did?   And don't you remember how you wouldn't let poor little Johnnie be baptised?
Well, I do hope your opinions have altered.   Eh, but
it's strange, it's strange, how two of your sons, and just
them two that you'd never set eyes on until this day,

should have made up their minds to go into the church!
And thanks to Johnnie there, they've been able to. If
I was to tell you all the struggles we've had, you
wouldn't believe me. They were clerks, and they might
have been clerks to this day, if it hadn't been for
Johnnie. But Johnnie could always earn money. It's
that engineering! And now Matthew's second curate at
St. Paul's and getting fifty pounds a year, and Henry'll
have a curacy next month at Bermondsey—it's been
promised, and all thanks to Johnnie!" She wept.

Johnnie, in the corner, who had so far done nought
but knock at the door, maintained stiffly his policy of
non-interference.

Priam Farll, angry, resentful, and quite untouched
by the recital, shrugged his shoulders. He was animated
by the sole desire to fly from the widow and progeny
of his late valet. But he could not fly. The Herculean
John was too close to the door. So he shrugged his
shoulders a second time.

"Yes, sir," said Matthew, "you may shrug your
shoulders, but you can't shrug us out of existence.
Here we are, and you can't get over us. You are our
father, and I presume that a kind of respect is due to
you. Yet how can you hope for our respect? Have
you earned it? Did you earn it when you ill-treated
our poor mother? Did you earn it when you left her,
with the most inhuman cruelty, to fend for herself in

the world? Did you earn it when you abandoned your children born and unborn? You are a bigamist, sir; a deceiver of women! Heaven knows——"

"Would you mind just toasting this bread?" Alice interrupted his impassioned discourse by putting the loaded toasting-fork into his hands, "while I make the tea?"

It was a novel way of stopping a mustang in full career, but it succeeded.

While somewhat perfunctorily holding the fork to the fire, Matthew glared about him, to signify his righteous horror, and other sentiments.

"Please don't burn it," said Alice gently. "Suppose you were to sit down on this footstool." And then she poured boiling water on the tea, put the lid on the pot, and looked at the clock to note the exact second at which the process of infusion had begun.

"Of course," burst out Henry, the twin of Matthew, "I need not say, madam, that you have all our sympathies. You are in a——"

"Do you mean me?" Alice asked.

In an undertone Priam could be heard obstinately repeating, "Never set eyes upon her before! Never set eyes on the woman before!"

"I do, madam," said Henry, not to be cowed nor deflected from his course. "I speak for all of us. You have our sympathies. You could not know the character of the man you married, or rather with whom you went through the ceremony of marriage. However, we have heard, by inquiry, that you made his acquaintance through the medium of a matrimonial agency; and indirectly, when one does that sort of thing, one takes one's chance. Your position is an extremely delicate one; but it is not too much to say that you brought it on yourself. In my work, I have encountered many sad instances of the result of lax moral principles; but I little thought to encounter the saddest of all in my own family. The discovery is just as great a blow to us as it is to you. We have suffered; my mother has suffered. And now, I fear, it is your turn to suffer. You are not this man's wife. Nothing can make you his wife. Yet you are living in the same house with him—under circumstances—er—without a chaperon. I hesitate to characterise your situation in plain words. It would scarcely become me, or mine, to do so. But really no lady could possibly find herself in a situation more false than—I am afraid there is only one word, open immorality, and—er—to put yourself right with society there is one thing, and only one, left for you to—er—do. I—I speak for the family, and I——"

"Sugar?" Alice questioned the mother of curates.

"Yes, please."

"One lump, or two?"

"Two, please."

"Speaking for the family——" Henry resumed.

"Will you kindly pass this cup to your mother?" Alice suggested.

Henry was obliged to take the cup. Excited by the fever of eloquence, he unfortunately upset it before it had reached his mother's hands.

"Oh, Henry!" murmured the lady, mournfully aghast. "You always were so clumsy! And a clean cloth, too!"

"Don't mention it, please," said Alice, and then to *her* Henry: "My dear, just run into the kitchen, and bring me something to wipe this up. Hanging behind the door—you'll see."

Priam sprang forward with astonishing celerity. And the occasion brooking no delay, the guardian of the portal could not but let him pass. In another moment the front door banged. Priam did not return. And Alice staunched the flow of tea with a clean, stiff serviette taken from the sideboard drawer.

A DEPARTURE.

The family of the late Henry Leek, each with a cup in hand, experienced a certain difficulty in maintaining the interview at the pitch set by Matthew and Henry.

Mrs. Leek, their mother, frankly gave way to soft tears, while eating bread-and-butter, jam and zebra-like toast. John took everything that Alice offered to him in gloomy and awkward silence.

"Does he mean to come back?" Matthew demanded at length. He had risen from the footstool.

"Who?" asked Alice.

Matthew paused, and then said, savagely and deliberately: "Father."

Alice smiled. "I'm afraid not. I'm afraid he's gone out. You see, he's a rather peculiar man. It's not the slightest use me trying to drive him. He can only be led. He has his good points—I can speak candidly as he isn't here, and I *will*—he has his good points. When Mrs. Leek, as I suppose she calls herself, spoke about his cruelty to her—well, I understood that. Far be it from me to say a word against him; he's often very good to me, but—another cup, Mr. John?"

John advanced to the table without a word, holding his cup.

"You don't mean to say, ma'am," said Mrs. Leek, "that he——?"

Alice nodded grievously.

Mrs. Leek burst into tears. "When Johnnie was barely five weeks old," she said, "he would twist my arm. And he kept me without money. And once he locked me up in the cellar. And one morning when I was ironing he snatched the hot iron out of my hand and——"

"Don't! Don't!" Alice soothed her. "I know. I know all you can tell me. I know because I've been through——"

"You don't mean to say he threatened *you* with the flat-iron?"

"If threatening was only all!" said Alice, like a martyr.

"Then he's not changed, in all these years!" wept the mother of curates.

"If he has, it's for the worse," said Alice. "How was I to tell?" she faced the curates. "How could I know? And yet nobody, nobody, could be nicer than he is at times!"

"That's true, that's true," responded the authentic Mrs. Henry Leek. "He was always so changeable, so queer."

"Queer!" Alice took up the word. "That's it. Queer! I don't think he's *quite* right in his head, not quite right. He has the very strangest fancies. I never take any notice of them, but they're there. I seldom get up in the morning without thinking, 'Well, perhaps to-day he'll have to be taken off.' "

"Taken off?"

"Yes, to Hanwell, or wherever it is. And you must remember " she said gazing firmly at the curates, "you've got his blood in your veins. Don't forget that. I suppose you want to make him go back to you, Mrs. Leek, as he certainly ought."

"Ye-es," murmured Mrs. Leek feebly.

"Well, if you can persuade him to go," said Alice, "if you can make him see his duty, you're welcome. But I'm sorry for you. I think I ought to tell you that this is my house, and my furniture. He's got nothing at all. I expect he never could save. Many's the blow he's laid on me in anger, but all the same I pity him. I pity him. And I wouldn't like to leave him in the lurch. Perhaps these three strong young men'll be able to do something with him. But I'm not sure. He's very strong. And he has a way of leaping out so sudden like."

Mrs. Leek shook her head as memories of the past rose up in her mind.

"The fact is," said Matthew sternly, "he ought to be prosecuted for bigamy. That's what ought to be done."

"Most decidedly," Henry concurred.

"You're quite right! You're quite right!" said Alice. "That's only justice. Of course he'd deny that he was the same Henry Leek. He'd deny it like anything. But in the end I daresay you'd be able to prove it. The worst of these law cases is they're so expensive. It means private detectives and all sorts of things, I be-

12*

lieve. Of course there'd be the scandal. But don't mind me! I'm innocent. Everybody knows me in Putney, and has done this twenty years. I don't know how it would suit you, Mr. Henry and Mr. Matthew, as clergymen, to have your own father in prison. That's as may be. But justice is justice, and there's too many men going about deceiving simple, trusting women. I've often heard such tales. Now I know they're all true. It's a mercy my own poor mother hasn't lived to see where I am to-day. As for my father, old as he was, if he'd been alive, there'd have been horse-whipping, that I do know."

After some rather pointless and disjointed remarks from the curates, a sound came from the corner near the door. It was John's cough.

"Better clear out of this!" John ejaculated. Such was his first and last oral contribution to the scene.

IN THE BATH.

Priam Farll was wandering about the uncharted groves of Wimbledon Common, and uttering soliloquies in language that lacked delicacy. He had rushed forth, in his haste, without an overcoat, and the weather was blusterously inclement. But he did not feel the cold; he only felt the keen wind of circumstance.

Soon after the purchase of his picture by the lunatic

landlord of a fully licensed house, he had discovered that the frame-maker in High Street knew a man who would not be indisposed to buy such pictures as he could paint, and transactions between him and the frame-maker had developed into a regular trade. The usual price paid for canvases was ten pounds, in cash. By this means he had earned about two hundred a year. No questions were put on either side. The paintings were delivered at intervals, and the money received; and Priam knew no more. For many weeks he had lived in daily expectation of an uproar, a scandal in the art-world, visits of police, and other inconveniences, for it was difficult to believe that the pictures would never come beneath the eye of a first-class expert. But nothing had occurred, and he had gradually subsided into a sense of security. He was happy; happy in the untrammelled exercise of his gift, happy in having all the money that his needs and Alice's demanded; happier than he had been in the errant days of his glory and his wealth. Alice had been amazed at his power of earning; and also, she had seemed little by little to lose her suspicions as to his perfect sanity and truthfulness. In a word, the dog of fate had slept; and he had taken particular care to let it lie. He was in that species of sheltered groove which is absolutely essential to the bliss of a shy and nervous artist, however great he may be.

And now this disastrous irruption, this resurrection of the early sins of the real Leek! He was hurt; he was startled; he was furious. But he was not surprised. The wonder was that the early sins of Henry Leek had not troubled him long ago. What could he do? He could do nothing. That was the tragedy: he could do nothing. He could but rely upon Alice. Alice was amazing. The more he thought of it, the more masterly her handling of these preposterous curates seemed to him. And was he to be robbed of this incomparable woman by ridiculous proceedings connected with a charge of bigamy? He knew that bigamy meant prison, in England. The injustice was monstrous. He saw those curates, and their mute brother, and the aggrieved mother of the three dogging him either to prison or to his deathbed! And how could he explain to Alice? Impossible to explain to Alice! . . . Still, it was conceivable that Alice would not desire explanation. Alice somehow never did desire an explanation. She always said, "I can quite understand," and set about preparing a meal. She was the comfortablest cushion of a creature that the evolution of the universe had ever produced.

Then the gusty breeze dropped and it began to rain. He ignored the rain. But December rain has a strange, horrid quality of chilly persistence. It is capable of conquering the most obstinate and serious mental preoccupation, and it conquered Priam's. It forced him to admit that his tortured soul had a fleshly garment and that the fleshly garment was soaked to the marrow. And his soul gradually yielded before the attack of the rain, and he went home.

He put his latchkey into the door with minute precautions against noise, and crept into his house like a thief, and very gently shut the door. Then, in the hall, he intently listened. Not a sound! That is to say, not a sound except the drippings of his hat on the linoleum. The sitting-room door was ajar. He timidly pushed it, and entered. Alice was darning stockings.

"Henry!" she exclaimed. "Why, you're wet through!" She rose.

"Have they cleared off?" he demanded.

"And you've been out without an overcoat! Henry, how could you? Well, I must get you into bed at once—instantly, or I shall have you down with pneumonia or something to-morrow!"

"Have they cleared off?" he repeated.

"Yes, of course," she said.

"When are they coming back?" he asked.

"I don't think they'll come back," she replied. "I think they've had enough. I think I've made them see that it's best to leave well alone. Did you ever see such toast as that curate made?"

"Alice, I assure you," he said, later—he was in a

boiling bath—"I assure you it's all a mistake. "I've never seen the woman before."

"Of course you haven't," she said calmingly. "Of course you haven't. Besides, even if you had, it serves her right. Everyone could see she's a nagging woman. And they seemed quite prosperous. They're hysterical —that's what's the matter with them, all of them—except the eldest, the one that never spoke. I rather liked him."

"But I *haven't!*" he reiterated, splashing his positive statement into the water.

"My dear, I know you haven't."

But he guessed that she was humouring him. He guessed that she was determined to keep him at all costs. And he had a disconcerting glimpse of the depths of utter unscrupulousness that sometimes disclose themselves in the mind of a good and loving woman.

"Only I hope there won't be any more of them!" she added dryly.

Ah! That was the point! He conceived the possibility of the rascal Leek having committed scores and scores of sins, all of which might come up against him. His affrighted vision saw whole regions populated by disconsolate widows of Henry Leek and their offspring, ecclesiastical and otherwise. He knew what Leek had been. Westminster Abbey was a strange goal for Leek to have achieved.

CHAPTER IX.

A GLOSSY MALE.

THE machine was one of those electric contrivances that do their work noiselessly and efficiently, like a garrotter or the guillotine. No odour, no teeth-disturbing grind of rack-and-pinion, no trumpeting, with that machine! It arrived before the gate with such absence of sound that Alice, though she was dusting in the front-room, did not hear it. She heard nothing till the bell discreetly tinkled. Justifiably assuming that the tinkler was the butcher's boy, she went to the door with her apron on, and even with the duster in her hand. A handsome, smooth man stood on the step, and the electric carriage made a background for him. He was a dark man, with curly black hair, and a moustache to match, and black eyes. His silk hat, of an incredible smooth newness, glittered over his glittering hair and eyes. His overcoat was lined with astrakan, and this important fact was casually betrayed at the lapels and at the sleeves. He wore a black silk necktie, with a small pearl pin in the mathematical centre of the perfect rhomboid of the upper part of a sailor's knot. His gloves were of slate colour. The chief characteristic of his faintly striped trousers was the crease, which seemed more than mortal. His boots were of *glacé* kid and as smooth as his cheeks. The cheeks had a fresh boyish colour, and between them, over admirable snowy teeth, projected the hooked key to this temperament. It is possible that Alice, from sheer thoughtlessness, shared the vulgar prejudice against Jews; but certainly she did not now feel it. The man's personal charm, his exceeding niceness, had always conquered that prejudice, whenever encountered. Moreover, he was only about thirty-five in years, and no such costly and beautiful male had ever yet stood on Alice's doorstep.

She at once, in her mind, contrasted him with the curates of the previous week, to the disadvantage of the Established Church. She did not know that this man was more dangerous than a thousand curates.

"Is this Mr. Leek's?" he inquired smilingly, and raised his hat.

"Yes," said Alice with a responsive smile.

"Is he in?"

"Well," said Alice, "he's busy at his work. You see in this weather he can't go out much—not to work —and so he——"

"Could I see him in his studio?" asked the glossy man, with the air of saying, "Can you grant me this supreme favour?"

It was the first time that Alice had heard the attic called a studio. She paused.

"It's about pictures," explained the visitor.

"Oh!" said Alice. "Will you come in?"

"I've run down specially to see Mr. Leek," said the visitor with emphasis.

Alice's opinion as to the seriousness of her husband's gift for painting had of course changed in two years. A man who can make two or three hundred a year by sticking colours anyhow, at any hazard, on canvasses—by producing alleged pictures that in Alice's secret view bore only a comic resemblance to anything at all—that man had to be taken seriously in his attic as an artisan. It is true that Alice thought the payment he received miraculously high for the quality of work done; but, with this agreeable Jew in the hall, and the *coupé* at the kerb, she suddenly perceived the probability of even greater miracles in the matter of price. She saw the average price of ten pounds rising to fifteen, or even twenty, pounds—provided her husband was given no opportunity to ruin the affair by his absurd, retiring shyness.

"Will you come this way?" she suggested briskly.

And all that elegance followed her up to the attic door: which door she threw open, remarking simply—

"Henry, here is a gentleman come to see you about pictures."

A CONNOISSEUR.

Priam recovered more quickly than might have been expected. His first thought was naturally that women are uncalculated, if not incalculable, creatures, and that the best of them will do impossible things—things inconceivable till actually done! Fancy her introducing a stranger, without a word of warning, direct into his attic! However, when he rose he saw the visitor's nose (whose nostrils were delicately expanding and contracting in the fumes of the oil-stove), and he was at once reassured. He knew that he would have to face neither rudeness, nor bluntness, nor lack of imagination, nor lack of quick sympathy. Besides, the visitor, with practical assurance, set the tone of the interview instantly.

"Good morning, *maître,*" he began, right off. "I must apologise for breaking in upon you. But I've come to see if you have any work to sell. My name is Oxford, and I'm acting for a collector."

He said this with a very agreeable mingling of sincerity, deference, and mercantile directness, also with a bright, admiring smile. He showed no astonishment at the interior of the attic.

Maître!

Well, of course, it would be idle to pretend that the

greatest artists do not enjoy being addressed as *maître*. 'Master' is the same word, but entirely different. It was a long time since Priam Farll had been called *maître*. Indeed, owing to his retiring habits, he had very seldom been called *maître* at all. A just-finished picture stood on an easel near the window; it represented one of the most wonderful scenes in London: Putney High Street at night; two omnibus horses stepped strongly and willingly out of a dark side street, and under the cold glare of the main road they somehow took on the quality of equestrian sculpture. The altercation of lights was in the highest degree complex. Priam understood immediately, from the man's calm glance at the picture, and the position which he instinctively took up to see it, that he was accustomed to looking at pictures. The visitor did not start back, nor rush forward, nor dissolve into hysterics, nor behave as though confronted by the ghost of a murdered victim. He just gazed at the picture, keeping his nerve and holding his tongue. And yet it was not an easy picture to look at. It was a picture of an advanced experimentalism, and would have appealed to nothing but the sense of humour in a person not a connoisseur.

"Sell!" exclaimed Priam. Like all shy men he could hide his shyness in an exaggerated familiarity. "What price this?" And he pointed to the picture.

There were no other preliminaries.

"It is excessively distinguished," murmured Mr. Oxford, in the accents of expert appreciation. "Excessively distinguished. May I ask how much?"

"That's what I'm asking you," said Priam, fiddling with a paint rag.

"Hum!" observed Mr. Oxford, and gazed in silence. Then: "Two hundred and fifty?"

Priam had virtually promised to deliver that picture to the picture-framer on the next day, and he had not expected to receive a penny more than twelve pounds for it. But artists are strange organisms.

He shook his head. Although two hundred and fifty pounds was as much as he had earned in the previous twelve months, he shook his grey head.

"No?" said Mr. Oxford kindly and respectfully, putting his hands behind his back. "By the way," he turned with eagerness to Priam, "I presume you have seen the portrait of Ariosto by Titian that they've bought for the National Gallery? What is your opinion of it, *maître?*" He stood expectant, glowing with interest.

"Except that it isn't Ariosto, and it certainly isn't by Titian, it's a pretty high-class sort of thing," said Priam.

Mr. Oxford smiled with appreciative content, nodding his head. "I hoped you would say so," he remarked. And swiftly he passed on to Segantini, then to J. W. Morrice, and then to Bonnard, demanding the *maître's* views.   In a few moments they were really discussing pictures.   And it was years since Priam had listened to the voice of informed commonsense on the subject of painting.   It was years since he had heard anything but exceeding puerility concerning pictures. He had, in fact, accustomed himself not to listen; he had excavated a passage direct from one ear to the other for such remarks.   And now he drank up the conversation of Mr. Oxford, and perceived that he had long been thirsty.   And he spoke his mind.   He grew warmer, more enthusiastic, more impassioned.   And Mr. Oxford listened with ecstasy.   Mr. Oxford had apparently a natural discretion.   He simply accepted Priam, as he stood, for a great painter.   No reference to the enigma why a great painter should be painting in an attic in Werter Road, Putney!   No inconvenient queries about the great painter's previous history and productions.   Just the frank, full acceptance of his genius!   It was odd, but it was comfortable.

"So you won't take two hundred and fifty?" asked Mr. Oxford, hopping back to business.

"No," said Priam sturdily.   "The truth is," he added, "I should rather like to keep that picture for myself."

"Will you take five hundred, *maître?*"

"Yes, I suppose I will," and Priam sighed.   A genuine sigh!   For he would really have liked to keep the picture.   He knew he had never painted a better.

"And may I carry it away with me?" asked Mr. Oxford.

"I expect so," said Priam.

"I wonder if I might venture to ask you to come back to town with me?" Mr. Oxford went on, in gentle deference. "I have one or two pictures I should very much like you to see, and I fancy they might give you pleasure. And we could talk over future business. If possibly you could spare an hour or so. If I might request——"

A desire rose in Priam's breast and fought against his timidity. The tone in which Mr. Oxford had said "I fancy they might give you pleasure" appeared to indicate something very much out of the common. And Priam could scarcely recollect when last his eyes had rested on a picture that was at once unfamiliar and great.

PARFITTS' GALLERIES.

I have already indicated that the machine was somewhat out of the ordinary. It was, as a fact, exceedingly out of the ordinary. It was much larger than electric carriages usually are. It had what the writers of "motoring notes" in papers written by the wealthy for the wealthy love to call a "limousine body." And outside and in, it was miraculously new and spotless.

On the ivory handles of its doors, on its soft yellow
leather upholstery, on its cedar woodwork, on its patent
blind apparatus, on its silver fittings, on its lamps, on
its footstools, on its silken arm-slings—not the minutest
trace of usage!   Mr. Oxford's car seemed to show that
Mr. Oxford never used a car twice, purchasing a new
car every morning, like stockbrokers their silk hats, or
the Duke of Selsea his trousers.   There was a table in
the "body" for writing, and pockets up and down devised to hold documents, also two armchairs, and a
suspended contrivance which showed the hour, the
temperature, and the fluctuations of the barometer;
there was also a speaking-tube.   One felt that if the
machine had been connected by wireless telegraphy with
the Stock Exchange, the leading studios and the Houses
of Parliament, and if a little restaurant had been con-
structed in the rear, Mr. Oxford might never have been
under the necessity of leaving the car; that he might
have passed all his days in it from morn to latest
eve.

The perfection of the machine and of Mr. Oxford's
attire and complexion caused Priam to look rather
shabby.   Indeed, he was rather shabby.   Shabbiness
had slightly overtaken him in Putney.   Once he had
been a dandy; but that was in the lamented Leek's
time.   And as the car glided, without smell and without
noise, through the encumbered avenues of London to-

wards the centre, now shooting forward like a star, now stopping with gentle suddenness, now swerving in a swift curve round a vehicle earthy and leaden-wheeled, Priam grew more and more uncomfortable. He had sunk into a groove at Putney. He never left Putney, save occasionally to refresh himself at the National Gallery, and thither he invariably went by train and tube, because the tube always filled him with wonder and romance, and always threw him up out of the earth at the corner of Trafalgar Square with such a strange exhilaration in his soul. So that he had not seen the main avenues of London for a long time. He had been forgetting riches and luxury, and the oriental cigarette-shops whose proprietors' names end in "opoulos," and the haughtiness of the ruling classes, and the still sterner haughtiness of their footmen. He had now abandoned Alice in Putney. And a mysterious demon seized him and gripped him, and sought to pull him back in the direction of the simplicity of Putney, and struggled with him fiercely, and made him writhe and shrink before the brilliant phenomena of London's centre, and indeed almost pitched him out of the car and set him running as hard as legs would carry to Putney. It was the demon which we call habit. He would have given a picture to be in Putney, instead of swimming past Hyde Park Corner to the accompaniment of Mr. Oxford's amiable and deferential and tactful conversation.

However, his other demon, shyness, kept him from imperiously stopping the car.

The car stopped itself in Bond Street, in front of a building with a wide archway, and the symbol of empire floating largely over its roof. Placards said that admission through the archway was a shilling; but Mr. Oxford, bearing Priam's latest picture as though it had cost fifty thousand instead of five hundred pounds, went straight into the place without paying, and Priam accepted his impressive invitation to follow. Aged military veterans whose breasts carried a row of medals saluted Mr. Oxford as he entered, and, within the penetralia, beings in silk hats as faultless as Mr. Oxford's raised those hats to Mr. Oxford, who did not raise his in reply. Merely nodded, Napoleonically! His demeanour had greatly changed. You saw here the man of unbending will, accustomed to use men as pawns in the chess of a complicated career. Presently they reached a private office where Mr. Oxford, with the assistance of a page, removed his gloves, furs, and hat, and sent sharply for a man who at once brought a frame which fitted Priam's picture.

"Do have a cigar," Mr. Oxford urged Priam, with a quick return to his earlier manner, offering a box in which each cigar was separately encased in gold-leaf. The cigar was such as costs a crown in a restaurant, half-a-crown in a shop, and twopence in Amsterdam.

13*

It was a princely cigar, with the odour of paradise and an ash as white as snow. But Priam could not appreciate it. No! He had seen on a beaten copper plate under the archway these words: "Parfitts' Galleries." He was in the celebrated galleries of his former dealers, whom by the way he had never seen. And he was afraid. He was mortally apprehensive, and had a sickly sensation in the stomach.

After they had scrupulously inspected the picture, through the clouds of incense, Mr. Oxford wrote out a cheque for five hundred pounds, and, cigar in mouth, handed it to Priam, who tried to take it with a casual air and did not succeed. It was signed "Parfitts'."

"I daresay you have heard that I'm now the sole proprietor of this place," said Mr. Oxford through his cigar.

"Really!" said Priam, feeling just as nervous as an inexperienced youth.

Then Mr. Oxford led Priam over thick carpets to a saloon where electric light was thrown by means of reflectors onto a small but incomparable band of pictures. Mr. Oxford had not exaggerated. They did give pleasure to Priam. They were not the pictures one sees every day, nor once a year. There was the finest Delacroix of its size that Priam had ever met with; also a Vermeer that made it unnecessary to visit the Rÿks Museum. And on the more distant wall, to which

Mr. Oxford came last, in a place of marked honour, was an evening landscape of Volterra, a hill-town in Italy. The bolts of Priam's very soul started when he caught sight of that picture. On the lower edge of the rich frame were two words in black lettering: "Priam Farll." How well he remembered painting it! And how masterfully beautiful it was!

"Now that," said Mr. Oxford, "is in my humble opinion one of the finest Farlls in existence. What do you think, Mr. Leek?"

Priam paused. "I agree with you," said he.

"Farll," said Mr. Oxford, "is about the only modern painter that can stand the company that that picture has in this room, eh?"

Priam blushed. "Yes," he said.

There is a considerable difference, in various matters, between Putney and Volterra; but the picture of Volterra and the picture of Putney High Street were obviously, strikingly, incontestably, by the same hand; one could not but perceive the same brushwork, the same masses, the same manner of seeing and of grasping, in a word the same dazzling and austere translation of nature. The resemblance jumped at one and shook one by the shoulders. It could not have escaped even an auctioneer. Yet Mr. Oxford did not refer to it. He seemed quite blind to it. All he said was, as

they left the room, and Priam finished his rather mono-
syllabic praise—

"Yes, that's the little collection I've just got together, and I am very proud to have shown it to
you. Now I want you to come and lunch with me at
my club. Please do. I should be desolated if you refused."

Priam did not care a halfpenny about the desolation of Mr. Oxford; and he most sincerely objected to
lunch at Mr. Oxford's club. But he said "Yes" because it was the easiest thing for his shyness to do,
Mr. Oxford being a determined man. Priam was afraid
to go. He was disturbed, alarmed, affrighted, by the
mystery of Mr. Oxford's silence.

They arrived at the club in the car.

THE CLUB.

Priam had never been in a club before. The statement may astonish, may even meet with incredulity,
but it is true. He had left the land of clubs early in
life. As for the English clubs in European towns, he
was familiar with their exteriors, and with the amiable
babble of their supporters at *tables d'hôte,* and his desire for further knowledge had not been so hot as to
inconvenience him. Hence he knew nothing of clubs.

Mr. Oxford's club alarmed and intimidated him; it

was so big and so black. Externally it resembled a
town-hall of some great industrial town. As you stood
on the pavement at the bottom of the flight of giant
steps that led to the first pair of swinging doors, your
head was certainly lower than the feet of a being who
examined you sternly from the other side of the glass.
Your head was also far below the sills of the mighty
windows of the ground-floor. There were two storeys
above the ground-floor, and above them a projecting
eave of carven stone that threatened the uplifted eye
like a menace. The tenth part of a slate, the merest
chip of a corner, falling from the lofty summit of that
pile, would have slain elephants. And all the façade
was black, black with ages of carbonic deposit. The
notion that the building was a town-hall that had got
itself misplaced and perverted gradually left you as you
gazed. You perceived its falseness. You perceived
that Mr. Oxford's club was a monument, a relic of the
days when there were giants on earth, that it had come
down unimpaired to a race of pigmies, who were making
the best of it. The sole descendant of the giants was
the scout behind the door. As Mr. Oxford and Priam
climbed towards it, this unique giant, with a giant's
force, pulled open the gigantic door, and Mr. Oxford
and Priam walked imperceptibly in, and the door swung
to with a large displacement of air. Priam found himself in an immense interior, under a distant carved

ceiling, far, far upwards, like heaven.   He watched Mr.
Oxford write his name in a gigantic folio, under a
gigantic clock.   This accomplished; Mr. Oxford led
him past enormous vistas to right and left, into a very
long chamber, both of whose long walls were studded
with thousands upon thousands of massive hooks—and
here and there upon a hook a silk hat or an overcoat.
Mr. Oxford chose a couple of hooks in the expanse,
and when they had divested themselves sufficiently he
led Priam forwards into another great chamber evidently
meant to recall the baths of Caracalla.   In gigantic
basins chiselled out of solid granite, Priam scrubbed
his finger-nails with a nail-brush larger than he had
previously encountered, even in nightmares, and an attendant brushed his coat with a utensil that resembled
a weapon of offence lately the property of Anak.

"Shall we go straight to the dining-room now," asked
Mr. Oxford, "or will you have a gin and angostura first?"

Priam declined the gin and angostura, and they
went up an overwhelming staircase of sombre marble,
and through other apartments to the dining-room,
which would have made an excellent riding-school.
Here one had six of the gigantic windows in a row,
each with curtains that fell in huge folds from the unseen into the seen.   The ceiling probably existed.   On
every wall were gigantic paintings in thick ornate
frames, and between the windows stood heroic busts of

marble set upon columns of basalt. The chairs would have been immovable had they not run on castors of weight-resisting rock, yet against the tables they had the air of negligible toys. At one end of the room was a sideboard that would not have groaned under an ox whole, and at the other a fire, over which an ox might have been roasted in its entirety, leaped under a mantel-piece upon which Goliath could not have put his elbows.

All was silent and grave; the floors were everywhere covered with heavy carpets which hushed all echoes. There was not the faintest sound. Sound, indeed, seemed to be deprecated. Priam had already passed the wide entrance to one illimitable room whose walls were clothed with warnings in gigantic letters: "Silence." And he had noticed that all chairs and couches were thickly padded and upholstered in soft leather, and that it was impossible to produce in them the slightest creak. At a casual glance the place seemed unoc-cupied, but on more careful inspection you saw midgets creeping about, or seated in easy-chairs that had ob-viously been made to hold two of them; these midgets were the members of the club, dwarfed into dolls by its tremendous dimensions. A strange and sinister race! They looked as though in the final stages of decay, and wherever their heads might rest was stretched a white cloth, so that their heads might not touch the spots sanctified by the heads of the mighty departed.

They rarely spoke to one another, but exchanged regards of mutual distrust and scorn; and if by chance
they did converse it was in tones of weary, brusque
disillusion. They could at best descry each other but
indistinctly in the universal pervading gloom—a gloom
upon which electric lamps, shining dimly yellow in their
vast lustres, produced almost no impression. The
whole establishment was buried in the past, dreaming
of its Titanic yore, when there were doubtless giants
who could fill those fauteuils and stick their feet on
those mantelpieces.

It was in such an environment that Mr. Oxford
gave Priam to eat and to drink off little ordinary plates
and out of tiny tumblers. No hint of the club's immemorial history in that excessively modern and excellent repast—save in the Stilton cheese, which seemed
to have descended from the fine fruity days of some
Homeric age, a cheese that Ulysses might have in-
augurated. I need hardly say that the total effect on
Priam's temperament was disastrous. (Yet how could
the diplomatic Mr. Oxford have guessed that Priam
had never been in a club before?) It induced in him
a speechless anguish, and he would have paid a sum
as gigantic as the club—he would have paid the very
cheque in his pocket—never to have met Mr. Oxford.
He was a far too sensitive man for a club, and his
moods were incalculable. Assuredly Mr. Oxford had

miscalculated the result of his club on Priam's humour; he soon saw his error.

"Suppose we take coffee in the smoking-room?" he said.

The populous smoking-room was the one part of the club where talking with a natural loudness was not a crime. Mr. Oxford found a corner fairly free from midgets, and they established themselves in it, and liqueurs and cigars accompanied the coffee. You could actually see midgets laughing outright in the mist of smoke; the chatter narrowly escaped being a din; and at intervals a diminutive boy entered and bawled the name of a midget at the top of his voice. Priam was suddenly electrified, and Mr. Oxford, very alert, noticed the electrification.

Mr. Oxford drank his coffee somewhat quickly, and then he leaned forward a little over the table, and put his moon-like face nearer to Priam's, and arranged his legs in a truly comfortable position beneath the table, and expelled a large quantity of smoke from his cigar. It was clearly the preliminary to a scene of confidence, the approach to the crisis to which he had for several hours been leading up.

Priam's heart trembled.

"What is your opinion, *maître*," he asked, "of the ultimate value of Farll's pictures?"

Priam was in misery. Mr. Oxford's manner was

deferential, amiable and expectant. But Priam did not
know what to say. He only knew what he would do if
he could have found the courage to do it: run away,
recklessly, unceremoniously, out of that club.

"I—I don't know," said Priam, visibly whitening.

"Because I've bought a goodish few Farlls in my
time," Mr. Oxford continued, "and I must say I've sold
them well. I've only got that one left that I showed
you this morning, and I've been wondering whether I
should stick to it and wait for a possible further rise, or
sell it at once."

"How much can you sell it for?" Priam mumbled.

"I don't mind telling you," said Mr. Oxford, "that
I fancy I could sell it for a couple of thousand. It's
rather small, but it's one of the finest in existence."

"I should sell it," said Priam, scarcely audible.

"You would? Well, perhaps you're right. It's a
question, in my mind, whether some other painter may
not turn up one of these days who would do that sort
of thing even better than Farll did it. I could imagine
the possibility of a really clever man coming along and
imitating Farll so well that only people like yourself,
maître, and perhaps me, could tell the difference. It's
just the kind of work that might be brilliantly imitated,
if the imitator was clever enough, don't you think?"

"But what do you mean?" asked Priam, perspiring
in his back.

"Well," said Mr. Oxford vaguely, "one never knows. The style might be imitated, and the market flooded with canvases practically as good as Farll's. Nobody might find it out for quite a long time, and then there might be confusion in the public mind, followed by a sharp fall in prices. And the beauty of it is that the public wouldn't really be any the worse. Because an imitation that no one can distinguish from the original is naturally as good as the original. You take me? There's certainly a tremendous chance for a man who could seize it, and that's why I'm inclined to accept your advice and sell my one remaining Farll."

He smiled more and more confidentially. His gaze was charged with a secret meaning. He seemed to be suggesting unspeakable matters to Priam. That bright face wore an expression which such faces wear on such occasions—an expression cheerfully insinuating that after all there is no right and no wrong—or at least that many things which the ordinary slave of convention would consider to be wrong are really right. So Priam read the expression.

"The dirty rascal wants me to manufacture imitations of myself for him!" Priam thought, full of sudden, hidden anger. "He's known all along that there's no difference between what I sold him and the picture he's already had. He wants to suggest that we should come to terms. He's simply been playing a game with me up to now." And he said aloud, "I don't know that I *advise* you to do anything. I'm not a dealer, Mr. Oxford."

He said it in a hostile tone that ought to have silenced Mr. Oxford for ever, but it did not. Mr. Oxford curved away, like a skater into a new figure, and began to expatiate minutely upon the merits of the Volterra picture. He analysed it in so much detail, and lauded it with as much justice, as though the picture was there before them. Priam was astonished at the man's exactitude. "Scoundrel! He knows a thing or two!" reflected Priam grimly.

"You don't think I overpraise it, do you, *cher maître?*" Mr. Oxford finished, still smiling.

"A little," said Priam.

If only Priam could have run away! But he couldn't! Mr. Oxford had him well in a corner. No chance of freedom! Besides, he was over fifty and stout.

"Ah! Now I was expecting you to say that! Do you mind telling me at what period you painted it?" Mr. Oxford inquired, very blandly, though his hands were clasped in a violent tension that forced the blood from the region of the knuckle-joints.

This was the crisis which Mr. Oxford had been leading up to! All the time Mr. Oxford's teethy smile had concealed a knowledge of Priam's identity!

CHAPTER X.

THE SECRET.

"WHAT do you mean?" asked Priam Farll. But he put the question weakly, and he might just as well have said, "I know what you mean, and I would pay a million pounds or so in order to sink through the floor." A few minutes ago he would only have paid five hundred pounds or so in order to run simply away. Now he wanted Maskelyne miracles to happen to him. The universe seemed to be caving in about the ears of Priam Farll.

Mr. Oxford was still smiling; smiling, however, as a man holds his breath for a wager. You felt that he could not keep it up much longer.

"You *are* Priam Farll, aren't you?" said Mr. Oxford in a very low voice.

"What makes you think I'm Priam Farll?"

"I think you are Priam Farll because you painted that picture I bought from you this morning, and I am sure that no one but Priam Farll could have painted it."

"Then you've been playing a game with me all morning!"

"Please don't put it like that, *cher maître,*" Mr. Oxford whisperingly pleaded. "I only wished to feel my ground. I know that Priam Farll is supposed to have been buried in Westminster Abbey. But for me the existence of that picture of Putney High Street, obviously just painted, is an absolute proof that he is not buried in Westminster Abbey, and that he still lives. It is an amazing thing that there should have been a mistake at the funeral, an utterly amazing thing, which involves all sorts of consequences! But that's not my business. Of course there must be clear reasons for what occurred. I am not interested in them—I mean not professionally. I merely argue, when I see a certain picture, with the paint still wet on it: 'That picture was painted by a certain painter. I am an expert, and I stake my reputation on it.' It's no use telling me that the painter in question died several years ago and was buried with national honours in Westminster Abbey. I say it couldn't have been so. I'm a connoisseur. And if the facts of his death and burial don't agree with the result of my connoisseurship, I say they aren't facts. I say there's been a—a misunderstanding about—er— corpses. Now, *cher maître,* what do you think of my position?" Mr. Oxford drummed lightly on the table.

"I don't know," said Priam. Which was another lie.

"You *are* Priam Farll, aren't you?" Mr. Oxford persisted.

"Well, if you will have it," said Priam savagely, "I am. And now you know!"

Mr. Oxford let his smile go. He had held it for an incredible time. He let it go, and sighed a gentle and profound relief. He had been skating over the thinnest ice, and had reached the bank amid terrific crackings, and he began to appreciate the extent of the peril braved. He had been perfectly sure of his con-noisseurship. But when one says one is perfectly sure, especially if one says it with immense emphasis, one always means "imperfectly sure." So it was with Mr. Oxford. And really, to argue, from the mere existence of a picture, that a tremendous deceit had been success-fully practised upon the most formidable of nations, implies rather more than rashness on the part of the arguer.

"But I don't want it to get about," said Priam, still in a savage whisper. "And I don't want to talk about it." He looked at the nearest midgets resentfully, suspecting them of eavesdropping.

"Precisely," said Mr. Oxford, but in a tone that lacked conviction.

"It's a matter that only concerns me," said Priam.

"Precisely," Mr. Oxford repeated. "At least it *ought* to concern only you. And I can't assure you too positively that I'm the last person in the world to want to pry; but——"

"You must kindly remember," said Priam, interrupting, "that you bought that picture this morning simply *as* a picture, on its merits. You have no authority to attach my name to it, and I must ask you not to do so."

"Certainly," agreed Mr. Oxford. "I bought it as a masterpiece, and I'm quite content with my bargain. I want no signature."

"I haven't signed my pictures for twenty years," said Priam.

"Pardon me," said Mr. Oxford. "Every square inch of every one is unmistakably signed. You could not put a brush on a canvas without signing it. It is the privilege of only the greatest painters not to put letters on the corners of their pictures in order to keep other painters from taking the credit for them afterwards. For me, all your pictures are signed. But there are some people who want more proof than connoisseurship can give, and that's where the trouble is going to be."

"Trouble?" said Priam, with an intensification of his misery.

"Yes," said Mr. Oxford. "I must tell you, so that you can understand the situation." He became very solemn, showing that he had at last reached the real point. "Some time ago a man, a little dealer, came to me and offered me a picture that I instantly recognised as one of yours. I bought it."

"How much did you pay for it?" Priam growled.

After a pause Mr. Oxford said, "I don't mind giving you the figure. I paid fifty pounds for it."

"Did you!" exclaimed Priam, perceiving that some person or persons had made four hundred per cent. on his work by the time it had arrived at a big dealer. "Who was the fellow?"

"Oh, a little dealer. Nobody. Jew, of course." Mr. Oxford's way of saying "Jew" was ineffably ironic. Priam knew that, being a Jew, the dealer could not be his frame-maker, who was a pure-bred Yorkshireman from Ravensthorpe. Mr. Oxford continued, "I sold that picture and guaranteed it to be a Priam Farll."

"The devil you did!"

"Yes. I had sufficient confidence in my judgment."

"Who bought it?"

"Whitney C. Witt, of New York. He's an old man now, of course. I expect you remember him, *cher maître.*" Mr. Oxford's eyes twinkled. "I sold it to him, and of course he accepted my guarantee. Soon afterwards I had the offer of other pictures obviously by you, from the same dealer. And I bought them. I kept on buying them. I daresay I've bought forty altogether."

"Did your little dealer guess whose work they were?" Priam demanded suspiciously.

"Not he! If he had done, do you suppose he'd

14*

have parted with them for fifty pounds apiece? Mind,
at first I thought I was buying pictures painted before
your supposed death. I thought, like the rest of the
world, that you were—in the Abbey. Then I began to
have doubts. And one day when a bit of paint came off
on my thumb, I can tell you I was startled. However,
I stuck to my opinion, and I kept on guaranteeing the
pictures as Farlls."

"It never occurred to you to make any inquiries?"

"Yes, it did," said Mr. Oxford. "I did my best to
find out from the dealer where he got the pictures from,
but he wouldn't tell me. Well, I sort of scented a
mystery. Now I've got no professional use for mysteries,
and I came to the conclusion that I'd better just let
this one alone. So I did."

"Well, why don't you keep on leaving it alone?"
Priam asked.

"Because circumstances won't let me. I sold
practically all those pictures to Whitney C. Witt. It
was all right. Anyhow I thought it was all right. I
put Parfitts' name and reputation on their being yours.
And then one day I heard from Mr. Witt that on the
back of the canvas of one of the pictures the name of
the canvas-makers, and a date, had been stamped, with a
rubber stamp, and that the date was after your supposed burial, and that his London solicitors had made
inquiries from the artist's-material people here, and these

people were prepared to prove that the canvas was made after Priam Farll's funeral. You see the fix?"

Priam did.

"My reputation—Parfitts'—is at stake. If those pictures aren't by you, I'm a swindler. Parfitts' name is gone for ever, and there'll be the greatest scandal that ever was. Witt is threatening proceedings. I offered to take the whole lot back at the price he paid me, without any commission. But he won't. He's an old man; a bit of a maniac I expect, and he won't. He's angry. He thinks he's been swindled, and what he says is that he's going to see the thing through. I've got to prove to him that the pictures are yours. I've got to show him what grounds I had for giving my guarantee. Well, to cut a long story short, I've found you, I'm glad to say!"

He sighed again.

"Look here," said Priam. "How much has Witt paid you altogether for my pictures?"

After a pause, Mr. Oxford said, "I don't mind giving you the figure. He's paid me seventy-two thousand pounds odd." He smiled, as if to excuse himself.

When Priam Farll reflected that he had received about four hundred pounds for those pictures—vastly less than one per cent. of what the shiny and prosperous dealer had ultimately disposed of them for, the

traditional fury of the artist against the dealer—of the
producer against the parasitic middleman—sprang into
flame in his heart.   Up till then he had never had any
serious cause of complaint against his dealers.   (Extremely successful artists seldom have.)   Now he saw
dealers, as the ordinary painters see them, to be the
authors of all evil!   Now he understood by what
methods Mr. Oxford had achieved his splendid car,
clothes, club, and minions.   These things were earned,
not by Mr. Oxford, but *for* Mr. Oxford in dingy studios,
even in attics, by shabby industrious painters!   Mr. Oxford was nothing but an opulent thief, a grinder of the
face of genius.   Mr. Oxford was, in a word, the spawn
of the devil, and Priam silently but sincerely consigned
him to his proper place.

It was excessively unjust of Priam.   Nobody had
asked Priam to die.   Nobody had asked him to give up
his identity.   If he had latterly been receiving tens
instead of thousands for his pictures, the fault was his
alone.   Mr. Oxford had only bought and only sold;
which was his true function.   But Mr. Oxford's sin, in
Priam's eyes, was the sin of having been right.

It would have needed less insight than Mr. Oxford
had at his disposal to see that Priam Farll was taking
the news very badly.

"For both our sakes, *cher maître,*" said Mr. Oxford
persuasively, "I think it will be advisable for you to put

me in a position to prove that my guarantee to Witt
was justified."

"Why for both our sakes?"

"Because, well, I shall be delighted to pay you, say
thirty-six thousand pounds in acknowledgment of—
er——" He stopped.

Probably he had instantly perceived that he was
committing a disastrous error of tact. Either he should
have offered nothing, or he should have offered the whole
sum he had received less a small commission. To suggest
dividing equally with Priam was the instinctive impulse,
the fatal folly, of a born dealer. And Mr. Oxford was
a born dealer.

"I won't accept a penny," said Priam. "And I
can't help you in any way. I'm afraid I must go now.
I'm late as it is."

His cold resistless fury drove him forward, and,
without the slightest regard for the amenities of clubs,
he left the table. Mr. Oxford, becoming more and
more the dealer, rose and followed him, even directed
him to the gigantic cloak-room, murmuring the while
soft persuasions and pacifications in Priam's ear.

"There may be an action in the courts," said Mr.
Oxford in the grand entrance hall, "and your testimony
would be indispensable to me."

"I can have nothing to do with it. Good day!"

The giant at the door could scarce open the

gigantic portal quickly enough for him.   He fled—fled,
surrounded by nightmare visions of horrible publicity in
a law-court.   Unthinkable tortures!   He damned Mr.
Oxford to the nethermost places, and swore that he
would not lift a finger to save Mr. Oxford from penal
servitude for life.

MONEY-GETTING.

He stood on the kerb of the monument, talking to
himself savagely.   At any rate he was safely outside
the monument, with its pullulating population of midgets
creeping over its carpets and lounging insignificant on
its couches.   He could not remember clearly what had
occurred since the moment of his getting up from the
table; he could not remember seeing anything or anyone on his way out; but he could remember the persuasive, deferential voice of Mr. Oxford following him
persistently as far as the giant's door.   In recollection
that club was like an abode of black magic to him; it
seemed so hideously alive in its deadness, and its doings
were so absurd and mysterious.   "Silence, silence!"
commanded the white papers in one vast chamber,
and, in another, babel existed!   And then that terrible
mute dining-room, with the high, unscalable mantelpieces that no midget could ever reach!   He kept uttering the most dreadful judgments on the club and on

Mr. Oxford, in quite audible tones, oblivious of the street. He was aroused by a rather scared man saluting him. It was Mr. Oxford's chauffeur, waiting patiently till his master should be ready to re-enter the wheeled salon. The chauffeur apparently thought him either demented or inebriated, but his sole duty was to salute, and he did nothing else.

Quite forgetting that this chauffeur was a fellow-creature, Priam immediately turned upon his heel, and hurried down the street. At the corner of the street was a large bank, and Priam, acquiring the reckless courage of the soldier in battle, entered the bank. He had never been in a London bank before. At first it reminded him of the club, with the addition of an enormous placard giving the day of the month as a mystical number—14—and other placards displaying solitary letters of the alphabet. Then he saw that it was a huge menagerie in which highly trained young men of assorted sizes and years were confined in stout cages of wire and mahogany. He stamped straight to a cage with a hole in it, and threw down the cheque for five hundred pounds—defiantly.

"Next desk, please," said a mouth over a high collar and a green tie, behind the grating, and a disdainful hand pushed the cheque back towards Priam.

"Next desk!" repeated Priam, dashed but furious.

"This is the A to M desk," said the mouth.

Then Priam understood the solitary letters, and he rushed, with a new accession of fury, to the adjoining cage, where another disdainful hand picked up the cheque and turned it over, with an air of saying, "Fishy, this!"

And, "It isn't endorsed!" said another mouth over another high collar and green tie. The second disdainful hand pushed the cheque back again to Priam, as though it had been a begging circular.

"Oh, if that's all!" said Priam, who could scarcely speak from anger. "Have you got such a thing as a pen?"

He was behaving in an extremely unreasonable manner. He had no right to visit his spleen on a perfectly innocent bank that paid twenty-five per cent. to its shareholders and a thousand a year each to its directors, and what trifle was left over to its men in cages. But Priam was not like you or me. He did not invariably act according to reason. He could not be angry with one man at once, nor even with one building at once. When he was angry he was inclusively and miscellaneously angry; and the sun, moon, and stars did not escape.

After he had endorsed the cheque the disdainful hand clawed it up once more, and directed upon its obverse and upon its reverse a battery of suspicions; then a pair of eyes glanced with critical distrust at so much of Priam's person as was visible. Then the eyes moved back, the mouth opened, in a brief word, and lo! there were four eyes and two mouths over the cheque, and four eyes for an instant on Priam. Priam expected someone to call for a policeman; in spite of himself he felt guilty—or anyhow dubious. It was the grossest insult to him to throw doubt on the cheque and to examine him in that frigid, shamelessly disillusioned manner.

"You *are* Mr. Leek?" a mouth moved.

"Yes" (very slowly).

"How would you like this?"

"I'll thank you to give it me in notes," answered Priam haughtily.

When the disdainful hand had counted twice every corner of a pile of notes, and had dropped the notes one by one, with a peculiar snapping sound of paper, in front of Priam, Priam crushed them together and crammed them without any ceremony and without gratitude to the giver, into the right pocket of his trousers. And he stamped out of the building with curses on his lips.

Still, he felt better, he felt assuaged. To cultivate and nourish a grievance when you have five hundred pounds in your pocket, in cash, is the most difficult thing in the world.

A VISIT TO THE TAILORS'.

He gradually grew calmer by dint of walking—
aimless, fast walking, with a rapt expression of the eyes
that on crowded pavements cleared the way for him
more effectually than a shouting footman. And then
he debouched unexpectedly onto the Embankment.
Dusk was already falling on the noble curve of the
Thames, and the mighty panorama stretched before
him in a manner mysteriously impressive which has
made poets of less poetic men than Priam Farll. Grand
hotels, offices of millionaires and of governments, grand
hotels, swards and mullioned windows of the law, grand
hotels, the terrific arches of termini, cathedral domes,
houses of parliament, and grand hotels, rose darkly
around him on the arc of the river, against the dark
violet murk of the sky. Huge trams swam past him
like glass houses, and hansoms shot past the trams and
automobiles past the hansoms; and phantom barges
swirled down on the full ebb, threading holes in bridges
as cotton threads a needle. It was London, and the
roar of London, majestic, imperial, super-Roman. And
lo! earlier than the earliest municipal light, an unseen
hand, the hand of destiny, printed a writing on the
wall of vague gloom that was beginning to hide the
opposite bank. And the writing said that Shipton's tea
was the best. And then the hand wiped largely out

that message and wrote in another spot that Mac-
donnell's whisky was the best; and so these two doctrines, in their intermittent pyrotechnics, continued to
give the lie to each other under the deepening night.
Quite five minutes passed before Priam perceived, between the altercating doctrines, the high scaffold-clad
summit of a building which was unfamiliar to him.   It
looked serenely and immaterially beautiful in the evening
twilight, and as he was close to Waterloo Bridge, his
curiosity concerning beauty took him over to the south
bank of the Thames.

After losing himself in the purlieus of Waterloo
Station, he at last discovered the rear of the building.
Yes, it was a beautiful thing; its tower climbed in
several coloured storeys, diminishing till it expired in a
winged figure on the sky.   And below, the building
was broad and massive, with a frontage of pillars over
great arched windows.   Two cranes stuck their arms
out from the general mass, and the whole enterprise
was guarded in a hedge of hoardings.   Through the
narrow doorway in the hoarding came the flare and the
hissing of a Wells's light.   Priam Farll glanced timidly
within. The interior was immense. In a sort of court of
honour a group of muscular, hairy males, silhouetted
against an illuminated lattice-work of scaffolding, were
chipping and paring at huge blocks of stone.   It was
a subject for a Rembrandt.

A fat untidy man meditatively approached the door-way. He had a roll of tracing papers in his hand, and the end of a long, thick pencil in his mouth. He was the man who interpreted the dreams of the architect to the dreamy British artisan. Experience of life had made him somewhat brusque.

"Look here," he said to Priam; "what the devil do you want?"

"What the devil do I want?" repeated Priam, who had not yet altogether fallen away from his mood of universal defiance. "I only want to know what the h—ll this building is."

The fat man was a little startled. He took his pencil from his mouth, and spat.

"It's the new Picture Gallery, built under the will of that there Priam Farll. I should ha' thought you'd ha' known that." Priam's lips trembled on the verge of an exclamation. "See that?" the fat man pursued, pointing to a small board on the hoarding. The board said, "No hands wanted."

The fat man coldly scrutinised Priam's appearance, from his greenish hat to his baggy creased boots.

Priam walked away.

He was dumfounded. Then he was furious again. He perfectly saw the humour of the situation, but it was not the kind of humour that induced rollicking laughter. He was furious, and employed the language of fury, when it is not overheard. Absorbed by his craft of painting, as in the old Continental days, he had long since ceased to read the newspapers, and though he had not forgotten his bequest to the nation, he had never thought of it as taking architectural shape. He was not aware of his cousin Duncan's activities for the perpetuation of the family name. The thing staggered him. The probabilities of the strange consequences of dead actions swept against him and overwhelmed him. Once, years ago and years ago, in a resentful mood, he had written a few lines on a piece of paper, and signed them in the presence of witnesses. Then nothing— nothing whatever— for two decades! The paper slept . . . and now this—this tremendous concrete result in the heart of London! It was incredible. It passed the bounds even of lawful magic.

His palace, his museum! The fruit of a captious hour!

Ah! But he was furious. Like every ageing artist of genuine accomplishment, he knew—none better—that there is no satisfaction save the satisfaction of fatigue after honest endeavour. He knew—none better—that wealth and glory and fine clothes are nought, and that striving is all. He had never been happier than during the last two years. Yet the finest souls have their re- actions, their rebellions against wise reason. And Priam's soul was in insurrection then. He wanted wealth and

glory and fine clothes once more. It seemed to him that
he was out of the world and that he must return to it.
The covert insults of Mr. Oxford rankled and stung.
And the fat foreman had mistaken him for a workman
cadging for a job.

He walked rapidly to the bridge and took a cab to
Conduit Street, where dwelt a firm of tailors with whose
Paris branch he had had dealings in his dandiacal
past.

An odd impulse perhaps, but natural.

A lighted clock-tower—far to his left as the cab
rolled across the bridge—showed that a legislative providence was watching over Israel.

ALICE ON THE SITUATION.

"I bet the building alone won't cost less than seventy
thousand pounds," he said.

He was back again with Alice in the intimacy of
Werter Road, and relating to her, in part, the adventures
of the latter portion of the day. He had reached home
long after tea-time; she, with her natural sagacity, had
not waited tea for him. Now she had prepared a rather
special tea for the adventurer, and she was sitting opposite to him at the little table, with nothing to do but
listen and refill his cup.

"Well," she said mildly, and without the least surprise at his figures, "I don't know what he could have been thinking of—your Priam Farll! I call it just silly. It isn't as if there wasn't enough picture-galleries already. When what there are are so full that you can't get in —then it will be time enough to think about fresh ones. I've been to the National Gallery twice, and upon my word I was almost the only person there! And it's free too! People don't *want* picture-galleries. If they did they'd go. Who ever saw a public-house empty, or Peter Robinson's? And you have to pay there! Silly, I call it! Why couldn't he have left his money to you, or at any rate to the hospitals, or something of that? No, it isn't silly. It's scandalous! It ought to be stopped!"

Now Priam had resolved that evening to make a serious, gallant attempt to convince his wife of his own identity. He was approaching the critical point. This speech of hers intimidated him, rather complicated his difficulties, but he determined to proceed bravely.

"Have you put sugar in this?" he asked.

"Yes," she said. "But you've forgotten to stir it. I'll stir it for you."

A charming wifely attention! It enheartened him.

"I say, Alice," he said, as she stirred, "you remember when first I told you I could paint?"

"Yes," she said.

"Well, at first you thought I was daft. You thought my mind was wandering, didn't you?"

"No," she said, "I only thought you'd got a bee in your bonnet." She smiled demurely.

"Well, I hadn't, had I?"

"Seeing the money you've made, I should just say you hadn't," she handsomely admitted. "Where we should be without it I don't know."

"You were wrong, weren't you? And I was right?"

"Of course," she beamed.

"And do you remember that time I told you I was really Priam Farll?"

She nodded, reluctantly.

"You thought I was absolutely mad. Oh, you needn't deny it! I could see well enough what your thoughts were."

"I thought you weren't quite well," she said frankly.

"But I was, my child. Now I've got to tell you again that I am Priam Farll. Honestly I wish I wasn't, but I am. The deuce of it is that that fellow that came here this morning has found it out, and there's going to be trouble. At least there has been trouble, and there may be more."

She was impressed. She knew not what to say.

"But, Priam——"

"He's paid me five hundred to-day for that picture I've just finished."

"Five hund——"

Priam snatched the notes from his pocket, and

with a gesture pardonably dramatic he bade her count them.

"Count them," he repeated, when she hesitated.

"Is it right?" he asked when she had finished.

"Oh, it's right enough," she agreed. "But, Priam, I don't like having all this money in the house. You ought to have called and put it in the bank."

"Dash the bank!" he exclaimed. "Just keep on listening to me, and try to persuade yourself I'm not mad. I admit I'm a bit shy, and it was all on account of that that I let that d—d valet of mine be buried as me."

"You needn't tell me you're shy," she smiled. "All Putney knows you're shy."

"I'm not so sure about that!" He tossed his head.

Then he began at the beginning and recounted to her in detail the historic night and morning at Selwood Terrace, with a psychological description of his feelings. He convinced her, in less than ten minutes, with the powerful aid of five hundred pounds in banknotes, that he in truth was Priam Farll.

And he waited for her to express an exceeding astonishment and satisfaction.

"Well, of course if you are, you are," she observed simply, regarding him with benevolent, possessive glances across the table. The fact was that she did not deal in names, she dealt in realities. He was her reality, and so long as he did not change visibly or actually— so long as he remained he—she did not much mind who he was. She added, "But I really don't know what you were *dreaming* of, Henry, to do such a thing!"

"Neither do I," he muttered.

Then he disclosed to her the whole chicanery of Mr. Oxford.

"It's a good thing you've ordered those new clothes," she said.

"Why?"

"Because of the trial."

"The trial between Oxford and Witt. What's that got to do with me?"

"They'll make you give evidence."

"But I sha'n't give evidence. I've told Oxford I'll have nothing to do with it at all."

"Suppose they make you? They can, you know, with a sub—sub something, I forget its name. Then you'll *have* to go in the witness-box."

"Me in the witness-box!" he murmured, undone.

"Yes," she said. "I expect it'll be very provoking indeed. But you'd want a new suit for it. So I'm glad you ordered one. When are you going to try on?"

CHAPTER XI.

AN ESCAPE.

ONE night, in the following June, Priam and Alice refrained from going to bed. Alice dozed for an hour or so on the sofa, and Priam read by her side in an easy-chair, and about two o'clock, just before the first beginnings of dawn, they stimulated themselves into a feverish activity beneath the parlour gas. Alice prepared tea, bread-and-butter, and eggs, passing briskly from room to room. Alice also ran upstairs, cast a few more things into a valise and a bag already partially packed, and, locking both receptacles, carried them downstairs. Meantime the whole of Priam's energy was employed in having a bath and in shaving. Blood was shed, as was but natural at that ineffable hour. While Priam consumed the food she had prepared, Alice was continually darting to and fro in the house. At one moment, after an absence, she would come into the parlour with a mouthful of hatpins; at another she would rush out to assure herself that the indispensable keys of the valise and bag with her purse were on the umbrella-stand, where they could not be forgotten.

Between her excursions she would drink thirty drops of tea.

"Now, Priam," she said at length, "the water's hot. Haven't you finished?   It'll be getting light soon."

"Water hot?" he queried, at a loss.

"Yes," she said.   "To wash up these things, of course.   You don't suppose I'm going to leave a lot of dirty things in the house, do you?   While I'm doing that you might stick labels on the luggage."

"They won't need to be labelled," he argued.   "We shall take them with us in the carriage."

"Oh, Priam," she protested, "how tiresome you are!"

"I've travelled more than you have."   He tried to laugh.

"Yes, and fine travelling it must have been, too! However, if you don't mind the luggage being lost, I don't."

During this she was collecting the crockery on a tray, with which tray she whizzed out of the room.

In ten minutes, hatted, heavily veiled, and gloved, she cautiously opened the front door and peeped forth into the lamplit street.   She peered to right and to left. Then she went as far as the gate and peered again.

"Is it all right?" whispered Priam, who was behind her.

"Yes, I think so," she whispered.

Priam came out of the house with the bag in one hand and the valise in the other, a pipe in his mouth, a stick under his arm, and an overcoat on his shoulder.

Alice ran up the steps, gazed within the house, pulled the door to silently, and locked it. Then beneath the summer stars she and Priam hastened furtively, as though the luggage had contained swag, up Werter Road towards Oxford Road. When they had turned the corner they felt very much relieved.

They had escaped.

It was their second attempt. The first, made in daylight, had completely failed. Their cab had been followed to Paddington Station by three other cabs containing the representatives and the cameras of three Sunday newspapers. A journalist had deliberately accompanied Priam to the booking office, had heard him ask for two seconds to Weymouth, and had bought a second to Weymouth himself. They had gone to Weymouth, but as within two hours of their arrival Weymouth had become even more impossible than Werter Road, they had ignominiously but wisely come back.

Werter Road had developed into the most celebrated thoroughfare in London. Its photograph had appeared in scores of newspapers, with a cross marking the abode of Priam and Alice. It was beset and infested by journalists of several nationalities from morn till night. Cameras were as common in it as lamp-posts. And a famous descriptive reporter of the *Sunday News* had got lodgings, at a high figure, exactly opposite Nr. 29. Priam and Alice could do nothing without publicity.

And if it would be an exaggeration to assert that evening papers appeared with Stop-press News: "5.40.
Mrs. Leek went out shopping," the exaggeration would
not be very extravagant. For a fortnight Priam had not
been beyond the door during daylight. It was Alice who,
alarmed by Priam's pallid cheeks and tightened nerves, had
devised the plan of flight before the early summer dawn.

They reached East Putney Station, of which the
gates were closed, the first workman's train being not
yet due. And there they stood. Not another human
being was abroad. Only the clock of St. Bude's was
faithfully awakening every soul within a radius of two
hundred yards each quarter of an hour. Then a porter
came and opened the gate—it was still exceedingly
early—and Priam booked for Waterloo in triumph.

"Oh," cried Alice, as they mounted the stairs, "I
quite forgot to draw up the blinds at the front of the
house." And she stopped on the stairs.

"What did you want to draw up the blinds for?"

"If they're down everybody will know instantly that
we've gone. Whereas if I—"

She began to descend the stairs.

"Alice!" he said sharply, in a strange voice. The
muscles of his white face were drawn.

"What?"

"D—n the blinds. Come along, or upon my soul
I'll kill you."

She realised that his nerves were in active insurrection, and that a mere nothing might bring about the fall of the government.

"Oh, very well!" She soothed him by her amiable obedience.

In a quarter of an hour they were safely lost in the wilderness of Waterloo, and the newspaper train bore them off to Bournemouth for a few days' respite.

THE NATION'S CURIOSITY.

The interest of the United Kingdom in the unique case of Witt v. Parfitts had already reached apparently the highest possible degree of intensity. And there was reason for the kingdom's passionate curiosity. Whitney Witt, the plaintiff, had come over to England, with his eccentricities, his retinue, his extreme wealth and his failing eyesight, specially to fight Parfitts. A half-pathetic figure, this white-haired man, once a connoisseur, who, from mere habit, continued to buy expensive pictures when he could no longer see them! Whitney Witt was implacably set against Parfitts, because he was convinced that Mr. Oxford had sought to take advantage of his blindness. There he was, conducting his action regardless of expense. His apartments and his regal daily existence at the Grand Babylon alone cost a fabulous sum, which may be precisely ascertained

by reference to illustrated articles in the papers. Then
Mr. Oxford, the youngish Jew who had acquired Parfitts, who was Parfitts, also cut a picturesque figure on
the face of London. He, too, was spending money with
both hands; for Parfitts itself was at stake. Last and
most disturbing, was the individual looming mysteriously
in the background, the inexplicable man who lived in
Werter Road, and whose identity would be decided by
the judgment in the case of Witt v. Parfitts. If Witt
won his action, then Parfitts might retire from business.
Mr. Oxford would probably go to prison for having sold
goods on false pretences, and the name of Henry Leek,
valet, would be added to the list of adventurous
scoundrels who have pretended to be their masters.
But if Witt should lose—then what a complication, and
what further enigmas to be solved! If Witt should
lose, the national funeral of Priam Farll had been a
fraudulent farce. A common valet lay under the hallowed
stones of the Abbey, and Europe had mourned in vain!
If Witt should lose, a gigantic and unprecedented
swindle had been practised upon the nation. Then the
question would arise, Why?

Hence it was not surprising that popular interest,
nourished by an indefatigable and excessively enterprising press, should have mounted till no one would
have believed that it could mount any more. But the
evasion from Werter Road on that June morning inten-

sified the interest enormously. Of course, owing to the drawn blinds, it soon became known, and the bloodhounds of the Sunday papers were sniffing along the platforms of all the termini in London. Priam's departure greatly prejudiced the cause of Mr. Oxford, especially when the bloodhounds failed and Priam persisted in his invisibility. If a man was an honest man, why should he flee the public gaze, and in the night? There was but a step from the posing of this question to the inevitable inference that Mr. Oxford's line of defence was really too fantastic for credence. Certainly organs of vast circulation, while repeating that, as the action was *sub judice,* they could say nothing about it, had already tried the action several times in their impartial columns, and they now tried it again, with the entire public as jury. And in three days Priam had definitely become a criminal in the public eye, a criminal flying from justice. Useless to assert that he was simply a witness subpenaed to give evidence at the trial! He had transgressed the unwritten law of the English constitution that a person prominent in a *cause célèbre* belongs for the time being, not to himself, but to the nation at large. He had no claim to privacy. In surreptitiously obtaining seclusion he was merely robbing the public and the public's press of their inalienable right.

Who could deny now the reiterated statement that he was a bigamist?

It came to be said that he must be on his way to
South America.   Then the public read avidly articles by
specially retained barristers on the extradition treaties with
Brazil, Argentina, Ecuador, Chili, Paraguay and Uruguay.

The curates Matthew and Henry preached to crowded
congregations at Putney and Bermondsey, and were re-
ported verbatim in the *Christian Voice Sermon Supple-
ment,* and other messengers of light.

And gradually the nose of England bent closer and
closer to its newspaper of a morning.   And coffee went
cold, and bacon fat congealed, from the Isle of Wight
to Hexham, while the latest rumours were being swallowed.   It promised to be stupendous, did the case of
Witt *v.* Parfitts.   It promised to be one of those cases
that alone make life worth living, that alone compensate
for the horrors of climate, in England.   And then the
day of hearing arrived, and the afternoon papers which
appear at nine o'clock in the morning announced that
Henry Leek (or Priam Farll, according to your wish)
and his wife (or his female companion and willing victim)
had returned to Werter Road.   And England held its
breath; and even Scotland paused, expectant; and Ire-
land stirred in its Celtic dream.

MENTION OF TWO MOLES.

The theatre in which the emotional drama of Witt
v. Parfitts was to be played, lacked the usual char-

acteristics of a modern place of entertainment. It was far too high for its width and breadth; it was badly illuminated; it was draughty in winter and stuffy in summer, being completely deprived of ventilation. Had it been under the control of the County Council it would have been instantly condemned as dangerous in case of fire, for its gangways were always encumbered and its exits of a mediæval complexity. It had no stage, no footlights, and all its seats were of naked wood except one.

This unique seat was occupied by the principal player, who wore a humorous wig and a brilliant and expensive scarlet costume. He was a fairly able judge, but he had mistaken his vocation; his rare talent for making third-rate jokes would have brought him a fortune in the world of musical comedy. His salary was a hundred a week; better comedians have earned less. On the present occasion he was in the midst of a double row of fashionable hats, and beneath the hats were the faces of fourteen feminine relatives and acquaintances. These hats performed the function of "dressing" the house. The principal player endeavoured to behave as though under the illusion that he was alone in his glory, but he failed.

There were four other leading actors: Mr. Pennington, K.C., and Mr. Vodrey, K.C., engaged by the plaintiff, and Mr. Cass, K.C., and Mr. Crepitude, K.C., engaged by the defendant. These artistes were the stars of their profession, nominally less glittering, but really far more glittering than the player in scarlet. Their wigs were of inferior quality to his, and their costumes shabby, but they did not mind, for whereas he got a hundred a week, they each got a hundred a day. Three junior performers received ten guineas a day apiece: one of them held a watching brief for the Dean and Chapter of the Abbey, who, being members of a Christian fraternity, were pained and horrified by the defendants' implication that they had given interment to a valet, and who were determined to resist exhumation at all hazards. The supers in the drama, whose business it was to whisper to each other and to the players, consisted of solicitors, solicitors' clerks, and experts; their combined emoluments worked out at the rate of a hundred and fifty pounds a day. Twelve excellent men in the jury-box received between them about as much as would have kept a K.C. alive for five minutes. The total expenses of production thus amounted to something like six or seven hundred pounds a day. The preliminary expenses had run into several thousands. The enterprise could have been made remunerative by hiring for it Covent Garden Theatre and selling stalls as for Tettrazzini and Caruso, but in the absurd auditorium chosen, crammed though it was to the perilous doors, the loss was necessarily terrific. Fortunately the affair was subsidised; not merely by the State, but also

by those two wealthy capitalists, Whitney C. Witt and
Mr. Oxford; and therefore the management were in a
position to ignore paltry financial considerations and to
practise art for art's sake.

In opening the case Mr. Pennington, K.C., gave instant proof of his astounding histrionic powers. He
began calmly, colloquially, treating the jury as friends
of his boyhood, and the judge as a gifted uncle, and
stated in simple language that Whitney C. Witt was
claiming seventy-two thousand pounds from the defendants, money paid for worthless pictures palmed off
upon the myopic and venerable plaintiff as masterpieces.
He recounted the life and death of the great painter
Priam Farll, and his solemn burial and the tears of the
whole world. He dwelt upon the genius of Priam Farll,
and then upon the confiding nature of the plaintiff.
Then he inquired who could blame the plaintiff for his
confidence in the uprightness of a firm with such a name
as Parfitts. And then he explained by what accident
of a dating-stamp on a canvas it had been discovered
that the pictures guaranteed to be by Priam Farll were
painted after Priam Farll's death.

He proceeded with no variation of tone: "The explanation is simplicity itself. Priam Farll was not really
dead. It was his valet who died. Quite naturally, quite
comprehensibly, the great genius Priam Farll wished to
pass the remainder of his career as a humble valet.

He deceived everybody; the doctor, his cousin, Mr. Duncan Farll, the public authorities, the Dean and Chapter of the Abbey, the nation—in fact, the entire world! As Henry Leek he married, and as Henry Leek he recommenced the art of painting—in Putney; he carried on the vocation several years without arousing the suspicions of a single person; and then—by a curious coincidence immediately after my client threatened an action against the defendant—he displayed himself in his true identity as Priam Farll. Such is the simple explanation," said Pennington, K.C., and added, "which you will hear presently from the defendant. Doubtless it will commend itself to you as experienced men of the world. You cannot but have perceived that such things are constantly happening in real life, that they are of daily occurrence. I am almost ashamed to stand up before you and endeavour to rebut a story so plausible and so essentially convincing. I feel that my task is well-nigh hopeless. Nevertheless, I must do my best."

And so on.

It was one of his greatest feats in the kind of irony that appeals to a jury. And the audience deemed that the case was already virtually decided.

After Whitney C. Witt and his secretary had been called and had filled the court with the echoing twang of New York (the controlled fury of the aged Witt was highly effective), Mrs. Henry Leek was invited to the witness-box. She was supported thither by her two curates, who, however, could not prevent her from weeping at the stern voice of the usher. She related her marriage.

"Is that your husband?" demanded Vodrey, K.C. (who had now assumed the principal *rôle,* Pennington, K.C., being engaged in another play in another theatre), pointing with one of his well-conceived dramatic gestures to Priam Farll.

"It is," sobbed Mrs. Henry Leek.

The unhappy creature believed what she said, and the curates, though silent, made a deep impression on the jury. In cross-examination, when Crepitude, K.C., forced her to admit that on first meeting Priam in his house in Werter Road she had not been quite sure of his identity, she replied—

"It's all come over me since. Shouldn't a woman recognise the father of her own children?"

"She should," interpolated the judge. There was a difference of opinion as to whether his word was jocular or not.

Mrs. Henry Leek was a touching figure, but not amusing. It was Mr. Duncan Farll who, quite unintentionally, supplied the first relief.

Duncan pooh-poohed the possibility of Priam being Priam. He detailed all the circumstances that followed the death in Selwood Terrace, and showed in fifty ways that Priam could not have been Priam. The man now masquerading as Priam was not even a gentleman,

whereas Priam was Duncan's cousin!   Duncan was an
excellent witness, dry, precise, imperturbable.   Under
cross-examination by Crepitude he had to describe particularly his boyish meeting with Priam.   Mr. Crepitude
was not inquisitive.

"Tell us what occurred," said Crepitude.

"Well, we fought."

"Oh! You fought! What did you two naughty boys
fight about?"   (Great laughter.)

"About a plum-cake, I think."

"Oh!   Not a seed-cake, a plum-cake?"   (Great
laughter.)

"I think a plum-cake."

"And what was the result of this sanguinary encounter?"   (Great laughter.)

"My cousin loosened one of my teeth."   (Great
laughter, in which the court joined.)

"And what did you do to him?"

"I'm afraid I didn't do much.   I remember tearing
half his clothes off."   (Roars of laughter, in which everyone joined except Priam and Duncan Farll.)

"Oh!   You are sure you remember that?   You are
sure that it wasn't he who tore *your* clothes off?"   (Lots
of hysteric laughter.)

"Yes," said Duncan, coldly dreaming in the past.
His eyes had the "far-away" look, as he added, "I remember now that my cousin had two little moles on his

neck below the collar. I seem to remember seeing them. I've just thought of it."

There is, of course, when it is mentioned in a theatre, something exorbitantly funny about even one mole. Two moles together brought the house down.

Mr. Crepitude leaned over to a solicitor in front of him; the solicitor leaned aside to a solicitor's clerk, and the solicitor's clerk whispered to Priam Farll, who nodded.

"Er——" Mr. Crepitude was beginning again, but he stopped and said to Duncan Farll, "Thank you. You can step down."

Then a witness named Justini, a cashier at the Hôtel de Paris, Monte Carlo, swore that Priam Farll, the renowned painter, had spent four days in the Hôtel de Paris one hot May, seven years ago, and that the person in the court whom the defendant stated to be Priam Farll was not that man. No cross-examination could shake Mr. Justini. Following him came the manager of the Hôtel Belvedere at Mont Pélerin, near Vevey, Switzerland, who related a similar tale and was equally unshaken.

And after that the pictures themselves were brought in, and the experts came after them and technical evidence was begun. Scarcely had it begun when a clock struck, and the performance ended for the day. The principal actors doffed their costumes, and snatched up the evening papers to make sure that the descriptive

16*

reporters had been as eulogistic of them as usual. The judge, who subscribed to a press-cutting agency, was glad to find, the next morning, that none of his jokes had been omitted by any of the nineteen chief London dailies. And the Strand and Piccadilly were quick with Witt *v.* Parfitts—on evening posters and in the strident mouths of newsboys. The telegraph wires vibrated to Witt *v.* Parfitts. In the great betting industrial towns of the provinces wagers were laid at scientific prices. England, in a word, was content, and the principal actors had the right to be content also. Very astute people in clubs and saloon bars talked darkly about those two moles, and Priam's nod in response to the whispers of the solicitor's clerk: such details do not escape the modern sketch writer at a thousand a year. To very astute people the two moles appeared to promise pretty things.

PRIAM'S REFUSAL.

"Leek in the box."

This legend got itself onto the telegraph wires and the placards within a few minutes of Priam's taking the oath. It sent a shiver of anticipation throughout the country. Three days had passed since the opening of the case (for actors engaged at a hundred a day for the run of the piece do not crack whips behind experts engaged at ten or twenty a day; the pace had therefore been dignified), and England wanted a fillip.

Nobody except Alice knew what to expect from Priam. Alice knew. She knew that Priam was in an extremely peculiar state which might lead to extremely peculiar results; and she knew also that there was nothing to be done with him! She herself had made one little effort to bathe him in the light of reason; the effort had not succeeded. She saw the danger of renewing it. Pennington, K.C., by the way, insisted that she should leave the court during Priam's evidence.

Priam's attitude towards the whole case was one of bitter resentment, a resentment now hot, now cold. He had the strongest possible objection to the entire affair. He hated Witt as keenly as he hated Oxford. All that he demanded from the world was peace and quietness, and the world would not grant him these inexpensive commodities. He had not asked to be buried in Westminster Abbey; his interment had been forced upon him. And if he chose to call himself by another name, why should he not do so? If he chose to marry a simple woman, and live in a suburb and paint pictures at ten pounds each, why should he not do so? Why should he be dragged out of his tranquillity because two persons in whom he felt no interest whatever, had quarrelled over his pictures? Why should his life have been made unbearable in Putney by the extravagant curiosity of a mob of journalists? And then, why should he be compelled, by means of a piece of blue paper, to go through the frightful ordeal and flame of publicity in a witness-box? That was the crowning un-merited torture, the unthinkable horror which had broken his sleep for many nights.

In the box he certainly had all the appearance of a trapped criminal, with his nervous movements, his restless lowered eyes, and his faint, hard voice that he could scarcely fetch up from his throat. Nervousness lined with resentment forms excellent material for the plastic art of a cross-examining counsel, and Pennington, K.C., itched to be at work. Crepitude, K.C., Oxford's counsel, was in less joyous mood. Priam was Crepitude's own witness, and yet a horrible witness, a witness who had consistently and ferociously declined to open his mouth until he was in the box. Assuredly he had nodded, in response to the whispered question of the solicitor's clerk, but he had not confirmed the nod, nor breathed a word of assistance during the three days of the trial. He had merely sat there, blazing in silence.

"Your name is Priam Farll?" began Crepitude.

"It is," said Priam sullenly, and with all the external characteristics of a liar. At intervals he glanced surrepti-tiously at the judge, as though the judge had been a bomb with a lighted fuse.

The examination started badly, and it went from worse to worse. The idea that this craven, prevaricat-ing figure in the box could be the illustrious, the world-

renowned Priam Farll, seemed absurd.   Crepitude had
to exercise all his self-control in order not to bully
Priam.

"That is all," said Crepitude, after Priam had given
his preposterous and halting explanations of the strange
phenomena of his life after the death of Leek.   None
of these carried conviction.   He merely said that the
woman Leek was mistaken in identifying him as her
husband; he inferred that she was hysterical; this inference alienated him from the audience completely.
His statement that he had no definite reason for pretending to be Leek—that it was an impulse of the moment—was received with mute derision.   His explanation, when questioned as to the evidence of the hotel officials, that more than once his valet Leek had gone about
impersonating his master, seemed grotesquely inadequate.

People wondered why Crepitude had made no reference to the moles.   The fact was, Crepitude was
afraid to refer to the moles.   In mentioning the moles
to Priam he might be staking all to lose all.

However, Pennington, K.C., alluded to the moles.
But not until he had conclusively proved to the judge,
in a cross-questioning of two hours' duration, that Priam
knew nothing of Priam's own youth, nor of painting,
nor of the world of painters.   He made a sad mess of
Priam.   And Priam's voice grew fainter and fainter,
and his gestures more and more self-incriminating.

Pennington, K. C., achieved one or two brilliant little effects.

"Now you say you went with the defendant to his club, and that he told you of the difficulty he was in!"

"Yes."

"Did he make you any offer of money?"

"Yes."

"Ah! What did he offer you?"

"Thirty-six thousand pounds." (Sensation in court.)

"So! And what was this thirty-six thousand pounds to be for?"

"I don't know."

"You don't know? Come now."

"I don't know."

"You accepted the offer?"

"No, I refused it." (Sensation in court.)

"Why did you refuse it?"

"Because I didn't care to accept it."

"Then no money passed between you that day?"

"Yes. Five hundred pounds."

"What for?"

"A picture."

"The same kind of picture that you had been selling at ten pounds?"

"Yes."

"So that on the very day that the defendant wanted you to swear that you were Priam Farll, the price of your pictures rose from ten pounds to five hundred?"

"Yes."

"Doesn't that strike you as odd?"

"Yes."

"You still say—mind, Leek, you are on your oath!—you still say that you refused thirty-six thousand pounds in order to accept five hundred."

"I sold a picture for five hundred."

(On the placards in the Strand: "Severe cross-examination of Leek.")

"Now about the encounter with Mr. Duncan Farll. Of course, if you are really Priam Farll, you remember all about that?"

"Yes."

"What age were you?"

"I don't know. About nine."

"Oh! You were about nine. A suitable age for cake." (Great laughter.) "Now, Mr. Duncan Farll says you loosened one of his teeth."

"I did."

"And that he tore your clothes."

"I daresay."

"He says he remembers the fact because you had two moles."

"Yes."

"Have you two moles?"

"Yes." (Immense sensation.)

Pennington paused.

"Where are they?"

"On my neck just below my collar."

"Kindly place your hand at the spot."

Priam did so. The excitement was terrific.

Pennington again paused. But, convinced that Priam
was an impostor, he sarcastically proceeded—

"Perhaps, if I am not asking too much, you will
take your collar off and show the two moles to the court?"

"No," said Priam stoutly. And for the first time he
looked Pennington in the face.

"You would prefer to do it, perhaps, in his lordship's room, if his lordship consents."

"I won't do it anywhere," said Priam.

"But surely——" the judge began.

"I won't do it anywhere, my lord," Priam repeated
loudly. All his resentment surged up once more; and
particularly his resentment against the little army of experts who had pronounced his pictures to be clever but
worthless imitations of himself. If his pictures, admittedly painted after his supposed death, could not
prove his identity; if his word was to be flouted by insulting and bewigged beasts of prey; then his moles
should not prove his identity. He resolved upon obstinacy.

"The witness, gentlemen," said Pennington, K.C., in
triumph to the jury, "has two moles on his neck, exactly

as described by Mr. Duncan Farll, but he will not display them!"

Eleven legal minds bent nobly to the problem whether the law and justice of England could compel a free man to take his collar off if he refused to take his collar off. In the meantime, of course, the case had to proceed. The six or seven hundred pounds a day must be earned, and there were various other witnesses. The next witness was Alice.

CHAPTER XII.

ALICE'S PERFORMANCES.

WHEN Alice was called, and when she stood up in the box, and, smiling indulgently at the doddering usher, kissed the book as if it had been a chubby nephew, a change came over the emotional atmosphere of the court, which felt a natural need to smile. Alice was in all her best clothes, but it cannot be said that she looked the wife of a super-eminent painter. In answer to a question she stated that before marrying Priam she was the widow of a builder in a small way of business, well known in Putney and also in Wandsworth. This was obviously true. She could have been nothing but the widow of a builder in a small way of business well known in Putney and also in Wandsworth. She was every inch that.

"How did you first meet your present husband, Mrs. Leek?" asked Mr. Crepitude.

"Mrs. Farll, if you please," she cheerfully corrected him.

"Well, Mrs. Farll, then."

"I must say," she remarked conversationally, "it seems queer you should be calling me Mrs. Leek, when they're paying you to prove that I'm Mrs. Farll, Mr.——, excuse me, I forget your name."

This nettled Crepitude, K.C. It nettled him, too, merely to see a witness standing in the box just as if she were standing in her kitchen talking to a tradesman at the door. He was not accustomed to such a spectacle. And though Alice was his own witness he was angry with her because he was angry with her husband. He blushed. Juniors behind him could watch the blush creeping like a tide round the back of his neck over his exceedingly white collar.

"If you'll be good enough to reply——" said he.

"I met my husband outside St. George's Hall, by appointment," said she.

"But before that. How did you make his acquaintance?"

"Through a matrimonial agency," said she.

"Oh!" observed Crepitude, and decided that he would not pursue that avenue. The fact was Alice had put him into the wrong humour for making the best of her. She was, moreover, in a very difficult position, for

Priam had positively forbidden her to have any speech
with solicitors' clerks or with solicitors, and thus Crepitude knew not what pitfalls for him her evidence might
contain. He drew from her an expression of opinion
that her husband was the real Priam Farll, but she
could give no reasons in support—did not seem to conceive that reasons in support were necessary.

"Has your husband any moles?" asked Crepitude
suddenly.

"Any what?" demanded Alice, leaning forward.

Vodrey, K.C., sprang up.

"I submit to your lordship that my learned friend is
putting a leading question," said Vodrey, K.C.

"Mr. Crepitude," said the judge, "can you not phrase
your questions differently?"

"Has your husband any birthmarks—er—on his
body?" Crepitude tried again.

"Oh! *Moles,* you said? You needn't be afraid.
Yes, he's got two moles, close together on his neck,
here." And she pointed amid silence to the exact spot.
Then, noticing the silence, she added, "That's all that
I *know* of."

Crepitude resolved to end his examination upon this
impressive note, and he sat down. And Alice had
Vodrey, K.C., to face.

"You met your husband through a matrimonial
agency?" he asked.

"Yes."

"Who first had recourse to the agency?"

"I did."

"And what was your object?"

"I wanted to find a husband, of course," she smiled. "What *do* people go to matrimonial agencies for?"

"You aren't here to put questions to me," said Vodrey severely.

"Well," she said, "I should have thought you would have known what people went to matrimonial agencies for. Still, you live and learn." She sighed cheerfully.

"Do you think a matrimonial agency is quite the nicest way of——"

"It depends what you mean by 'nice,'" said Alice.

"Womanly."

"Yes," said Alice shortly, "I do. If you're going to stand there and tell me I'm unwomanly, all I have to say is that you're unmanly."

"You say you first met your husband outside St. George's Hall?"

"Yes."

"Never seen him before?"

"No."

"How did you recognise him?"

"By his photograph."

"Oh, he'd sent you his photograph?"

"Yes."

"With a letter?"

"Yes."

"In what name was the letter signed?"

"Henry Leek."

"Was that before or after the death of the man who was buried in Westminster Abbey?"

"A day or two before." (Sensation in court.)

"So that your present husband was calling himself Henry Leek before the death?"

"No, he wasn't. That letter was written by the man that died. My husband found my reply to it, and my photograph, in the man's bag afterwards; and happening to be strolling past St. George's Hall just at the moment like——"

"Well, happening to be strolling past St. George's Hall just at the moment like——" (Titters).

"I caught sight of him and spoke to him. You see, I thought then that he was the man who wrote the letter."

"What made you think so?"

"I had the photograph."

"So that the man who wrote the letter and died didn't send his own photograph. He sent another photograph—the photograph of your husband?"

"Yes, didn't you know that? I should have thought you'd have known that."

"Do you really expect the jury to believe that tale?"

Alice turned smiling to the jury. "No," she said,

"I'm not sure as I do.   I didn't believe it myself for a long time.   But it's true."

"Then at first you didn't believe your husband was the real Priam Farll?"

"No.   You see, he didn't exactly tell me like.   He only sort of hinted."

"But you didn't believe?"

"No."

"You thought he was lying?"

"No, I thought it was just a kind of an idea he had. You know my husband isn't like other gentlemen."

"I imagine not," said Vodrey.   "Now, when did you come to be perfectly sure that your husband was the real Priam Farll?"

"It was the night of that day when Mr. Oxford came down to see him.   He told me all about it then."

"Oh!   That day when Mr. Oxford paid him five hundred pounds?"

"Yes."

"Immediately Mr. Oxford paid him five hundred pounds you were ready to believe that your husband was the real Priam Farll.   Doesn't that strike you as excessively curious?"

"It's just how it happened," said Alice blandly.

"Now about these moles. You pointed to the right side of your neck. Are you sure they aren't on the left side?"

"Let me think now," said Alice, frowning.   "When

he's shaving in a morning—he gets up earlier now than he used to—I can see his face in the looking-glass, and in the looking-glass the moles are on the left side. So on *him* they must be on the right side. Yes, the right side. That's it."

"Have you never seen them except in a mirror, my good woman?" interpolated the judge.

For some reason Alice flushed. "I suppose you think that's funny," she snapped, slightly tossing her head.

The audience expected the roof to fall. But the roof withstood the strain, thanks to a sagacious deafness on the part of the judge. If, indeed, he had not been visited by a sudden deafness, it is difficult to see how he would have handled the situation.

"Have you any idea," Vodrey inquired, "why your husband refuses to submit his neck to the inspection of the court?"

"I didn't know he had refused."

"But he has."

"Well," said Alice, "if you hadn't turned me out of the court while he was being examined, perhaps I could have told you. But I can't as it is. So it serves you right."

Thus ended Alice's performances.

THE PUBLIC CAPTIOUS.

The court rose, and another six or seven hundred pounds was gone into the pockets of the celebrated

artistes engaged.   It became at once obvious, from the
tone of the evening placards and the contents of evening papers, and the remarks in crowded suburban trains,
that for the public the trial had resolved itself into an
affair of moles.   Nothing else now interested the great
and intelligent public.   If Priam had those moles on his
neck, then he was the real Priam.   If he had not, then
he was a common cheat.   The public had taken the
matter into its own hands.   The sturdy commonsense
of the public was being applied to the affair.   On the
whole it may be said that the sturdy commonsense of
the public was against Priam.   For the majority, the
entire story was fishily preposterous.   It must surely be
clear to the feeblest brain that if Priam possessed moles
he would expose them.   The minority, who talked of
psychology and the artistic temperament, were regarded
as the cousins of Little Englanders and the direct
descendants of pro-Boers.

Still, the thing ought to be proved or disproved.

Why didn't the judge commit him for contempt of
court?   He would then be sent to Holloway and be
compelled to strip—and there you were!

Or why didn't Oxford hire someone to pick a
quarrel with him in the street and carry the quarrel to
blows, with a view to raiment-tearing?

A nice thing, English justice—if it had no machinery

to force a man to show his neck to a jury! But then English justice *was* notoriously comic.

And whole trainfuls of people sneered at their country's institution in a manner which, had it been adopted by a foreigner, would have plunged Europe into war and finally tested the blue-water theory. Undoubtedly the immemorial traditions of English justice came in for very severe handling, simply because Priam would not take his collar off.

And he would not.

The next morning there were consultations in counsel's rooms, and the common law of the realm was ransacked to find a legal method of inspecting Priam's moles, without success. Priam arrived safely at the courts with his usual high collar, and was photographed thirty times between the kerb and the entrance hall.

"He's slept in it!" cried wags.

"Bet yer two ter one it's a clean 'un!" cried other wags. "His missus gets his linen up."

It was subject to such indignities that the man who had defied the Supreme Court of Judicature reached his seat in the theatre. When solicitors and counsel attempted to reason with him, he answered with silence. The rumour ran that in his hip pocket he was carrying a revolver wherewith to protect the modesty of his neck.

The celebrated artistes, having perceived the folly of losing six or seven hundred pounds a day because

Priam happened to be an obstinate idiot, continued with the case. For Mr. Oxford and another army of experts of European reputation were waiting to prove that the pictures admittedly painted after the burial in the National Valhalla, were painted by Priam Farll, and could have been painted by no other. They demonstrated this by internal evidence. In other words, they proved by deductions from squares of canvas that Priam had moles on his neck. It was a phenomenon eminently legal. And Priam, in his stiff collar, sat and listened. The experts, however, achieved two feats, both unintentionally. They sent the judge soundly to sleep, and they wearied the public, which considered that the trial was falling short of its early promise. This *expertise* went on to the extent of two whole days and appreciably more than another thousand pounds. And on the third day Priam, somewhat hardened to renown, reappeared with his mysterious neck, and more determined than ever. He had seen in a paper, which was otherwise chiefly occupied with moles and experts, a cautious statement that the police had collected the necessary *primâ facie* evidence of bigamy, and that his arrest was imminent. However, something stranger than arrest for bigamy happened to him.

NEW EVIDENCE.

The principal King's Bench corridor in the Law

Courts, like the other main corridors, is a place of strange meetings and interviews. A man may receive there a bit of news that will change the whole of the rest of his life, or he may receive only an invitation to a mediocre lunch in the restaurant underneath; he never knows beforehand. Priam assuredly did not receive an invitation to lunch. He was traversing the crowded thoroughfares—for with the exception of match and toothpick sellers the corridor has the characteristics of a Strand pavement in the forenoon—when he caught sight of Mr. Oxford talking to a woman. Now, he had exchanged no word with Mr. Oxford since the historic scene in the club, and he was determined to exchange no word; however, they had not gone through the formality of an open breach. The most prudent thing to do, therefore, was to turn and take another corridor. And Priam would have fled, being capable of astonishing prudence when prudence meant the avoidance of unpleasant encounters; but, just as he was turning, the woman in conversation with Mr. Oxford saw him, and stepped towards him with the rapidity of thought, holding forth her hand. She was tall, thin, and stiffly distinguished in the brusque, Dutch-doll motions of her limbs. Her coat and skirt were quite presentable; but her feet were large (not her fault, of course, though one is apt to treat large feet as a crime), and her feathered hat was even larger. She hid her age behind a veil.

"How do you do, Mr. Farll?" she addressed him firmly, in a voice which nevertheless throbbed.

It was Lady Sophia Entwistle.

"How do you do?" he said, taking her offered hand.

There was nothing else to do, and nothing else to say.

Then Mr. Oxford put out his hand.

"How do you do, Mr. Farll?"

And, taking Mr. Oxford's hated hand, Priam said again, "How do you do?"

It was all just as if there had been no past; the past seemed to have been swallowed up in the ordinariness of the crowded corridor. By all the rules for the guidance of human conduct, Lady Sophia ought to have denounced Priam with outstretched dramatic finger to the contempt of the world as a philanderer with the hearts of trusting women; and he ought to have kicked Mr. Oxford along the corridor for a scheming Hebrew. But they merely shook hands and asked each other how they did, not even expecting an answer. This shows to what extent the ancient qualities of the race have deteriorated.

Then a silence.

"I suppose you know, Mr. Farll," said Lady Sophia, rather suddenly, "that I have got to give evidence in this case."

"No," he said, "I didn't."

"Yes, it seems they have scoured all over the Continent in vain to find people who knew you under your proper name, and who could identify you with certainty, and they couldn't find one—doubtless owing to your peculiar habits of travel."

"Really," said Priam.

He had made love to this woman. He had kissed her. They had promised to marry each other. It was a piece of wild folly on his part; but, in the eyes of an impartial person, folly could not excuse his desertion of her, his flight from her intellectual charms. His gaze pierced her veil. No, she was not quite so old as Alice. She was not more plain than Alice. She certainly knew more than Alice. She could talk about pictures without sticking a knife into his soul and turning it in the wound. She was better dressed than Alice. And her behaviour on the present occasion, candid, kind, correct, could not have been surpassed by Alice. And yet . . . Her demeanour was without question prodigiously splendid in its ignoring of all that she had gone through. And yet . . . Even in that moment of complicated misery he had enough strength to hate her because he had been fool enough to make love to her. No excuse whatever for him, of course!

"I was in India when I first heard of this case," Lady Sophia continued. "At first I thought it must be a sort of Tichborne business over again. Then, knowing you as I did, I thought perhaps it wasn't."

"And as Lady Sophia happens to be in London now," put in Mr. Oxford, "she is good enough to give her invaluable evidence on my behalf."

"That is scarcely the way to describe it," said Lady Sophia coldly. "I am only here because you compel me to be here by subpœna. It is all due to your acquaintanceship with my aunt."

"Quite so, quite so!" Mr. Oxford agreed. "It naturally can't be very agreeable to you to have to go into the witness-box and submit to cross-examination. Certainly not. And I am the more obliged to you for your kindness, Lady Sophia."

Priam comprehended the situation. Lady Sophia, after his supposed death, had imparted to relatives the fact of his engagement, and the unscrupulous scoundrel, Mr. Oxford, had got hold of her and was forcing her to give evidence for him. And after the evidence, the joke of every man in the street would be to the effect that Priam Farll, rather than marry the skinny spinster, had pretended to be dead.

"You see," Mr. Oxford added to him, "the important point about Lady Sophia's evidence is that in Paris she saw both you and your valet—the valet obviously a servant, and you obviously his master. There can, therefore, be no question of her having been deceived by the valet posing as the master. It is a most fortunate thing that by a mere accident I got on the tracks of Lady Sophia in time. In the nick of time. Only yesterday afternoon!"

No reference by Mr. Oxford to Priam's obstinacy in the matter of collars. He appeared to regard Priam's collar as a phenomenon of nature, such as the weather, or a rock in the sea, as something to be accepted with resignation! No sign of annoyance with Priam! He was the prince of diplomatists, was Mr. Oxford.

"Can I speak to you a minute?" said Lady Sophia to Priam.

Mr. Oxford stepped away with a bow.

And Lady Sophia looked steadily at Priam. He had to admit again that she was stupendous. She was his capital mistake; but she was stupendous.

At their last interview he had embraced her. She had attended his funeral in Westminster Abbey. And she could suppress all that from her eyes! She could stand there calm and urbane in her acceptance of the terrific past. Apparently she forgave.

Said Lady Sophia simply, "Now, Mr. Farll, shall I have to give evidence or not? You know it depends on you?"

The casualness of her tone was sublime; it was heroic; it made her feet small.

He had sworn to himself that he would be cut in pieces before he would aid the unscrupulous Mr. Oxford by removing his collar in presence of those dramatic artistes. He had been grossly insulted, disturbed, mal-treated, and exploited. The entire world had meddled with his private business, and he would be cut in pieces before he would display those moles which would decide the issue in an instant.

Well, she had cut him in pieces.

"Please don't worry," said he in reply. "I will attend to things."

At that moment Alice, who had followed him by a later train, appeared.

"Good morning, Lady Sophia," he said, raising his hat, and left her.

THOUGHTS ON JUSTICE.

"Farll takes his collar off." "Witt *v.* Parfitts. Result." These and similar placards flew in the Strand breezes. Never in the history of empires had the removal of a starched linen collar (size $16\frac{1}{2}$) created one-thousandth part of the sensation caused by the removal of this collar. It was an epoch-making act. It finished the drama of Witt *v.* Parfitts. The renowned artistes engaged did not, of course, permit the case to collapse at once. No, it had to be concluded slowly and majestically, with due forms and expenses. New witnesses (such as doctors) had to be called, and old ones recalled. Duncan Farll, for instance, had to be recalled, and if the situation was ignominious for Priam

it was also ignominious for Duncan. Duncan's sole
advantage in his defeat was that the judge did not skin
him alive in the summing up, nor the jury in their ver-
dict. England breathed more freely when the affair
was finally over and the renowned artistes engaged had
withdrawn enveloped in glory. The truth was that
England, so proud of her systems, had had a fright.
Her judicial methods had very nearly failed to make a
man take his collar off in public. They had really
failed, but it had all come right in the end, and so
England pretended that they had only just missed failing. A grave injustice would have been perpetrated
had Priam chosen not to take off his collar. People
said, naturally, that imprisonment for bigamy would
have included the taking-off of collars; but then it was
rumoured that prosecution for bigamy had not by any
means been a certainty, as since leaving the box Mrs.
Henry Leek had wavered in her identification. However, the justice of England had emerged safely. And
it was all very astounding and shocking and improper.
And everybody was exceedingly wise after the event.
And with one voice the press cried that something painful ought to occur at once to Priam Farll, no matter
how great an artist he was.

The question was: How could Priam be trapped in
the net of the law? He had not committed bigamy.
He had done nothing. He had only behaved in a

negative manner.   He had not even given false information to the registrar.   And Dr. Cashmore could
throw no light on the episode, for he was dead.   His
wife and daughters had at last succeeded in killing him.
The judge had intimated that the ecclesiastical wrath of
the Dean and Chapter might speedily and terribly over-
take Priam Farll; but that sounded vague and unsatisfactory to the lay ear.

In short, the matter was the most curious that ever
was.   And for the sake of the national peace of mind,
the national dignity, and the national conceit, it was
allowed to drop into forgetfulness after a few days.
And when the papers announced that, by Priam's wish,
the Farll museum was to be carried to completion and
formally conveyed to the nation, despite all, the nation
decided to accept that honourable amend, and went off
to the seaside for its annual holiday.

THE WILL TO LIVE.

Alice insisted on it, and so, immediately before their
final departure from England, they went.   Priam pretended that the visit was undertaken solely to please
her; but the fact is that his own morbid curiosity moved
in the same direction.   They travelled by an omnibus
past the Putney Empire and the Walham Green Empire
as far as Walham Green, and there changed into another one which carried them past the Chelsea Empire,

the Army and Navy Stores, and the Hotel Windsor to the doors of Westminster Abbey. And they vanished out of the October sunshine into the beam-shot gloom of Valhalla. It was Alice's first view of Valhalla, though of course she had heard of it. In old times she had visited Madame Tussaud's and the Tower, but she had not had leisure to get round as far as Valhalla. It impressed her deeply. A verger pointed them to the nave; but they dared not demand more minute instructions. They had not the courage to ask for *It.* Priam could not speak. There were moments with him when he could not speak lest his soul should come out of his mouth and flit irrecoverably away. And he could not find the tomb. Save for the outrageous tomb of mighty Newton, the nave seemed to be as naked as when it came into the world. Yet he was sure he was buried in the nave—and only three years ago, too! Astounding, was it not, what could happen in three years? He knew that the tomb had not been removed, for there had been an article in the *Daily Record* on the previous day asking in the name of a scandalised public whether the Dean and Chapter did not consider that three months was more than long enough for the correction of a fundamental error in the burial department. He was gloomy; he had in truth been somewhat gloomy ever since the trial. Perhaps it was the shadow of the wrath of the Dean and Chapter on him. He had

ceased to procure joy in the daily manifestations of life
in the streets of the town.   And this failure to discover
the tomb intensified the calm, amiable sadness which
distinguished him.

Alice, gazing around, chiefly with her mouth, inquired suddenly—

"What's that printing there?"

She had detected a legend incised on one of the
small stone flags which form the vast floor of the nave.
They stooped over it.   "PRIAM FARLL," it said simply,
in fine Roman letters and then his dates.   That was
all.   Near by, on other flags, they deciphered other
names of honour.   This austere method of marking the
repose of the dead commended itself to him, caused
him to feel proud of himself and of the ridiculous England that somehow keeps our great love.   His gloom
faded.   And do you know what idea rushed from his
heart to his brain?   "By Jove!   I will paint finer
pictures than any I've done yet!"   And the impulse to
recommence the work of creation surged over him.   The
tears started to his eyes.

"I like that!" murmured Alice, gazing at the stone.
"I do think that's nice."

And *he* said, because he truly felt it, because the
will to live raged through him again, tingling and
smarting:

"I'm glad I'm not there."

They smiled at each other, and their instinctive hands fumblingly met.

A few days later, the Dean and Chapter, stung into action by the majestic rebuke of the *Daily Record,* amended the floor of Valhalla and caused the mortal residuum of the immortal organism known as Henry Leek to be nocturnally transported to a different bed.

ON BOARD.

A few days later, also, a North German Lloyd steamer quitted Southampton for Algiers, bearing among its passengers Priam and Alice. It was a rough starlit night, and from the stern of the vessel the tumbled white water made a pathway straight to receding England. Priam had come to love the slopes of Putney with the broad river at the foot; but he showed what I think was a nice feeling in leaving England. His sojourn in our land had not crowned him with brilliance. He was not a being created for society, nor for cutting a figure, nor for exhibiting tact and prudence in the crises of existence. He could neither talk well nor read well, nor express himself in exactly suitable actions. He could only express himself at the end of a brush. He could only paint extremely beautiful pictures. That was the major part of his vitality. In minor ways he may have been, upon occasions, a fool. But he was never a fool on canvas. He said everything there, and said it to perfection, for those who could read, for those who can read, and for those who will be able to read five hundred years hence. Why expect more from him? Why be disappointed in him? One does not expect a wire-walker to play fine billiards. You yourself, mirror of prudence that you are, would have certainly avoided all Priam's manifold errors in the conduct of his social career; but, you see, he was divine in another way.

As the steamer sped along the lengthening pathway from England, one question kept hopping in and out of his mind:

"I wonder what they'll do with me next time?"

Do not imagine that he and Alice were staring over the stern at the singular isle. No! There were imperative reasons, which affected both of them, against that. It was only in the moments of the comparative calm which always follows insurrections, that Priam had leisure to wonder, and to see his own limitations, and joyfully to meditate upon the prospect of age devoted to the sole doing of that which he could so supremely, in a sweet exile with the enchantress, Alice.

THE END.

PRINTING OFFICE OF THE PUBLISHER.

www.ingramcontent.com/pod-product-compliance
Lightning Source LLC
Chambersburg PA
CBHW071309200626
46813CB00015B/791